It reads like a Hollywood script!

Yohanna

I'm not looking for romance. I'd rather just focus on my career; it's what I'm good at. Love? Not so much.

Lukkas

It's been years since I've dated—legitimately. Yes, the paparazzi have shot me with beautiful women, but they're just photo ops. (*shaking his head vehemently*) I'm not looking for love. Not me! Not again!

Yohanna's mom

I tell her all the time, "Get married!
It'll solve all your problems!" (*breathing exasperatedly*)
But does she listen? When is she going to learn that Mother knows best?

The Matchmaking Mamas

We haven't met a bachelor or bachelorette we can't match. (*smiling sweetly into the camera*) Today: single... Tomorrow: in love!

This is what the critics are saying:
"Finding your soul mate has never been so much fun!"

Dear Reader,

The Matchmaking Mamas are at it again. All three of these vital ladies who are determined to make the most of the second half of their lives have their own companies to keep them busy, but they are far more interested in, and gratified by, what they do as a sideline. Bringing people together does not ultimately bring any extra money into their pockets, but it does make their hearts swell. Because, after all, isn't love the most important thing there is? With it, you can scale mountains; without it, nothing really matters at the end of the day no matter what your title is or how much money you have.

This time around, the ladies have decided to bring together a supercharged type-A dynamo who has just lost her job through no fault of her own, and a highly successful movie producer who is still grieving over the wife he lost almost three years ago. Granted, the coupling is a challenge, but the ladies love nothing better than a good challenge—unless, of course, it's attending the wedding that inevitably follows.

I hope this latest installment of the matchmaking ladies entertains you. If it does, then my work here is done. As always, I thank you for taking the time to read this, and from the bottom of my heart, I wish you someone to love who loves you back.

Best,

Marie Ferrarella

Her Red-Carpet Romance

Marie Ferrarella

 HARLEQUIN® SPECIAL EDITION®

Recycling programs
for this product may
not exist in your area.

ISBN-13: 978-0-373-65891-6

Her Red-Carpet Romance

Copyright © 2015 by Marie Rydzynski-Ferrarella

Printed in U.S.A.

USA TODAY bestselling and RITA® Award-winning author **Marie Ferrarella** has written more than two hundred books for Harlequin, some under the name Marie Nicole. Her romances are beloved by fans worldwide. Visit her website, marieferrarella.com.

Books by Marie Ferrarella

Harlequin Special Edition

Matchmaking Mamas

Diamond in the Ruff
Dating for Two
Wish Upon a Matchmaker
Ten Years Later...
A Perfectly Imperfect Match
Once Upon a Matchmaker

The Fortunes of Texas: Cowboy Country

Mendoza's Secret Fortune

The Fortunes of Texas: Welcome to Horseback Hollow

Lassoed by Fortune

The Fortunes of Texas: Southern Invasion

A Small Fortune

Montana Mavericks: Back in the Saddle

Real Vintage Maverick

Harlequin Romantic Suspense

Mission: Cavanaugh Baby
Cavanaugh on Duty
A Widow's Guilty Secret
Cavanaugh's Surrender
Cavanaugh Rules

Visit the Author Profile page at Harlequin.com for more titles.

To
Mary-Theresa Hussey
in loving
gratitude
for all the good years

Prologue

Cecilia Parnell reached into her pocket to take out the key her client had given her, then stopped midway and pulled her hand out again.

The initial movement had been automatic. She had the keys to all of her clients' homes. Ninety percent of her clients were at work when she and her cleaning crew arrived; the other 10 percent usually preferred to be out when their homes were rendered spotless from top to bottom.

A firm believer in boundaries and privacy, Cecilia made it a policy never to use the key when she knew her client would be home. And today Yohanna Andrzejewski was home. She knew that because the young woman had specifically requested to see her.

Cecilia assumed the request had something to do with some sort of dissatisfaction with the quality of the work her crew did. If so, this would be a first, since no one had *ever* registered any complaints, not in all the years that she had been in this business.

Pressing the doorbell, Cecilia took a step back from the condo door so that Yohanna could see her when she looked through the peephole.

But it was obvious that her client didn't bother checking to see who was there. The door opened immediately, giving Cecilia the impression that the young woman was standing right behind the front door, waiting for her to arrive.

"Thank you for coming, Mrs. Parnell," Yohanna said, closing the door behind her. She sounded breathless, as if she'd been running.

Or perhaps crying.

"Of course, dear—" Cecilia replied kindly.

She was about to say something else when she turned and really looked at the young woman for the first time. Yohanna, usually so bright and upbeat that she practically sparkled, not only looked solemn but almost drained of all color, as well. Cecilia stopped walking. The mother in her instantly kicked in.

"What's wrong, dear?" she asked, concerned.

Yohanna took a deep breath and then let it out. It sounded almost like a mournful sigh. "I—I'm afraid that I have to let you go," she murmured, appearing stricken and exceedingly uncomfortable.

For the life of her Cecilia couldn't think of a single reason why she and her crew were being dismissed. She screened every one of her people very carefully before she hired them. Her daughter was a private investigator, so background checks were very easy to run. All of her employees had been with her for at least two years if not longer, and each one of them did excellent work.

Something else was going on.

"May I ask why?"

Yohanna's eyes widened as she realized the natural implication of what she had just said. She was quick to correct the misunderstanding.

"Oh, no, it's not anything that you or your crew have done. If anything, they're even better than when you first started cleaning here. I'm really thrilled with the job you've been doing."

Confusion creased Cecilia's brow. "Then, I don't understand. If you're happy with our work, why are you letting us go?" The moment Cecilia asked the question, she saw the tears shining in the younger woman's intense blue eyes. "Oh, darling, what's wrong?" she repeated.

This time, not standing on any formality, Cecilia took the young woman into her arms and hugged her, offering her mute comfort as well as a shoulder to cry on.

Ordinarily, Yohanna kept her problems to herself. She didn't like burdening other people, especially when there was nothing they could do to help or change the situation. But this time, she felt so overwhelmed, so helpless, not to mention betrayed, the words just came spilling out.

"I was laid off yesterday," Yohanna told the sympathetic woman. "I can't afford to pay you."

It was obvious that uttering the words was excruciating for Yohanna.

Cecilia gently guided the young woman to the light gray sofa and sat with her.

"Don't worry about paying me. You've been a wonderful client for four years. We'll work something out.

That's not important now. Tell me exactly what happened," Cecilia coaxed.

Yohanna took another deep breath, as if that could somehow shield her from the wave of pain that came with the words. Being laid off was a whole new experience for her and she felt awful.

"Mr. McGuire sold the company to Walters & Sons," she told Cecilia, referring to the man who had owned the company where she had worked. "The deal went through two days ago, before any of us knew about it. Their head of Human Resources called me into her office yesterday morning and said that they wouldn't be needing my services since they already had someone who could do my job."

Cecilia could just imagine how hard that must have been for the young woman to hear. One moment the future looked bright and secure, the next there was nothing around her but chaos and upheavals.

"That's simply awful," Cecilia sympathized. "Let me make you some tea and you can tell me everything." She rose from the sofa. "Did you know any of this was coming?" Cecilia asked as she walked into the kitchen.

Yohanna followed, looking, in Cecilia's estimation, like a lost puppy trying to find its way home.

"No, I didn't. None of us did," she said, referring to some of the other people she worked with. "I went to work for the company the year before I graduated college. Nine years. I was there nine years," she proclaimed. "McGuire's was like home to me. More," she emphasized, and then added in a quiet voice, "No one there berated me for not having a love life."

Cecilia took a wild guess as to the source of the berating Yohanna was referring to. It wasn't really much of a stretch. "Not like your mother does?"

Yohanna nodded and pressed her lips together, trying to get hold of herself. "I'm sorry I'm such a mess," she apologized, "but I just got off the phone with her."

Admittedly, when she'd told her mother about being suddenly laid off, she'd been hoping for a positive suggestion. Or, at the very least, sympathy. She'd received neither. "My mother's solution for everything is to get married."

"She just wants to see you happy," Cecilia told her as she filled the kettle with water from the tap.

"She just wants grandchildren," Yohanna contradicted. "I don't think she'd care if I married Godzilla as long as she got grandchildren out of it."

An amused smile played on Cecilia's lips. "The subsequent grandchildren from that union would be much too hairy for her liking," she quipped. Placing the kettle on the stove, she switched on the burner beneath it.

"But the immediate problem right now is to get you back into the work force." Cecilia had never been one to beat around the bush. That was for people like Maizie Sommers and Theresa Manetti, her two best friends since the third grade. They were far more delicate and eloquent in their approach to things. She had always been more of a blunt straight shooter. "What is it you do again, dear?"

"A little bit of everything and anything. Make sure that everything is running smoothly, keep track of appointments, meetings, suppliers. Make calls... In short, I guess you could call me an organizer. I take—took," she corrected herself, "care of all the details and made sure that everything at the office was running smoothly."

Cecilia nodded, the wheels in her head turning quickly. "I know people who know people who know people," she said, making something vague sound positive. "Let me make a few calls. We'll see if we can't get you back in the game."

In more ways than one, Cecilia thought. *Wait until I tell the girls we might have another project on our hands.* The mention of the young woman's mother's mindset had not gone unnoticed.

"You really think so?" Yohanna asked, brightening a little. "I'd be eternally grateful for anything you can do to help."

Cecilia smiled at the young woman. "Leave it to me," she promised confidently. Among all the people she and her friends currently knew—and that was a lot, given the nature of their businesses—there had to be someone who could use a sharp young go-getter like Yohanna.

Just then, the kettle emitted a high-pitched whistle. The tea was brewed.

"Ah, I believe it's playing our song," Cecilia said cheerfully, crossing back to the stove. In her head she was already calling Maizie and Theresa. They were going to want to hear all about Yohanna and her present predicament. "Everything's going to be just fine, dear," she promised, filling the teacup to the brim. "You just wait and see."

"I hope so," Yohanna murmured. But at the present moment she was having trouble mustering enthusiasm.

Chapter One

"You know, for a man who currently has the number one movie at the box office for the past three weeks, you really don't look very happy," Theresa Manetti commented to her client as she paused for a moment to stand by Lukkas Spader.

In the catering business for more than twelve years now, Theresa quickly surveyed the large room where she was presently catering the popular producer's impromptu party, a last-minute send-off that he was throwing for his departing assistant, Janice Brooks.

Tall, with broad shoulders and a broader smile— a smile that was conspicuously absent at the moment, Theresa noted—the thirty-six-year-old wunderkind, as those in higher places tended to dub him, shrugged.

"I can't rest on my laurels, Theresa. In this cutthroat business, you're only as good as your next project."

Theresa narrowed her eyes as she studied the young man. That wasn't at the heart of his problem. She could tell by the lost look in his eyes.

"There's something else, isn't there?" the woman asked. "Don't bother denying it, Lukkas. I raised two silver-tongued lawyers, I can see beyond the facade. You're young, good-looking—I'm old so I'm allowed to say that—and the world is currently at your feet. Yet you look as if you've just lost your best friend. What's bothering you?"

Lukkas shrugged. Admitting that the woman had guessed correctly wasn't going to cost him anything. Besides, he liked this woman whose catering service he'd used half a dozen times or so. There was something about Theresa Manetti that reminded him of his late mother.

"You're not old," he told her and then grew more serious when he said, "She's leaving."

"She," Theresa repeated, looking around the room to see if she could spot the woman Lukkas was talking about.

He nodded. "Jan."

Theresa looked at him in surprise. "You mean the young woman you threw the going-away party for?"

She couldn't see them as a pair, but if he didn't want this Jan leaving, why was he throwing this party for her? Why wasn't he trying to convince the young woman to stay?

Lukkas frowned as he nodded. "She's following her heart and marrying some guy in England she met while we were in production on *My Wild Irish Rose.*" As if a lightbulb had suddenly gone off in his head, he realized what his caterer was probably thinking. That this was a matter of the heart. Nothing could have been further from the truth.

"Don't get me wrong," he said, quickly setting Theresa straight. "I'm happy that Jan's happy, but I don't know what I'm going to do without her."

"Why?" Theresa asked, curious. "What is it that she does?"

"She keeps me honest and organized," he told her with a dry laugh. Because the woman was still looking at him, waiting for a viable answer, Lukkas elaborated, "I'm the one with the ideas and the energy, the inspiration. Jan's the one who makes sense of it all, who simplifies my chaos and makes sure that everything gets done on time."

Aware of the level of work involved in what Lukkas did, that certainly sounded like a taxing job, Theresa thought.

"And you don't have anyone to take her place?" she ventured. At the same time Theresa realized this wasn't a matter involving the heart. Lukkas seemed genuinely happy that his assistant had found someone to love so this wasn't something that could be fixed with a good match.

A pity, she silently lamented. She and her friends hadn't had a good challenge in almost a month. All three of them ran their own respective businesses, but nothing truly made them come to life like pairing up a couple and moving their lives along; lives that would have otherwise just gone their own separate routes, never bumping into one another, never discovering the pot of gold that was waiting for them at the end of the rainbow.

Thinking of that made her recall the poker game she and her friends had played last Monday. The card game was really just an excuse to get together, unwind and oc-

casionally talk about a possible new opportunity for them
to play Cupid. Last Monday, Cecilia had spent most of
her time talking about a young woman named Yohanna
Something-or-other—the last name was a tongue twister
at best. Apparently the young woman had just lost her
job and was also too sweet and adorable—Cecilia's exact
words—to be without a soul mate.

"Jan is going to be hard, if not impossible, to replace,"
Lukkas was saying.

Theresa smiled at the much-sought-after producer.
He was single. He was exceedingly handsome. He was
perfect. "Don't be too sure," she said.

He turned toward her. "You *know* someone?"

Theresa's smile was warm and genuine—and very
encouraging. "Dear boy, I *always* know someone." Theresa's eyes were fairly sparkling at this point.

Watching her, Lukkas thought that this woman must
have a trick or two up her sleeve. Right now, he needed
to find someone to replace Jan. A competent someone.
"Tell me more. I'm listening."

A little less than twenty-four hours later Yohanna
Andrzejewski found herself standing on Lukkas Spader's doorstep. *The* Lukkas Spader, big-time producer of
some very special movies.

Part of her thought she was dreaming. The other part
was exceedingly nervous. That was the part that had allowed her knees to feel like Jell-O.

Taking a deep breath and telling herself to calm down,
she leaned over and rang the doorbell. And then smiled.
The doorbell played several bars from the first movie
the producer had ever made: *Dreamland.*

She closed her eyes, recalling the rest of the score.

And that was the way Lukkas first saw her, standing on his doorstep, her eyes shut and swaying to some inner tune.

"Can I help you?"

The voice was deep and sexy. Startled, her eyes flew open.

The man was even better looking than his pictures, she realized as she frantically went in search of her tongue. It, along with her brain, had gone missing in action. It took a second for her to bring about the reunion.

"I'm—" She had to clear her throat before continuing. "Yohanna Andrzejewski. I'm here about the job opening," she added after a beat.

He'd been expecting her. Glancing at his watch, he saw that she was early. A hopeful sign, he thought. "I've been expecting you," he told her. "Follow me."

She fell into step behind him. "You answered your own door," she noted, slightly surprised.

"Had to," he told her. "It hasn't learned to open itself."

She laughed. "I was surprised that you have a house in Newport Beach," she confessed. "You're not all that far from where I live." Initially anticipating a long commute for the interview, she'd been relieved when she was told that he would see her in his Orange County home.

"Things are a little chaotic here," he admitted. "I haven't finished getting all the furniture yet. I think of this as my home away from home. Don't get me wrong, I love Hollywood." Entering a first-floor bedroom he'd converted into an office, Lukkas crossed to his desk, took a seat and gestured for her to take a seat on the opposite side. "But sometimes you just have to get away from the noise just so you're able to hear yourself think."

"Yes, sir," Yohanna responded.

The smile on her lips was almost shy. He was amused but also somewhat skeptical about whether this petite, attractive young woman was equal to the job he needed doing.

"I noticed on your résumé that your last job was with a law firm." He raised an eyebrow as he took a closer look at the dark blonde sitting before him. "Are you a lawyer?" He was aware that most law school graduates had to begin at the bottom of the heap if they were even lucky enough to land a position with *any* firm.

"No, sir."

"Don't do that," he told her.

She hadn't a clue what he might be referring to. "Do what, sir?"

"Call me sir," he specified. "You make me feel like my father—not exactly a feeling I cherish," he added more or less to himself.

Even so, she'd heard him. "Sorry, si—Mr. Spader." She'd managed to catch herself.

"Even worse," he told her. "My name is Lukkas. Think you can manage that?" Yohanna nodded vigorously. "Good," he pronounced.

Letting her résumé fall to his desk, he moved his chair in closer and leaned over, creating a feeling of intimacy. "So tell me, Yohanna with-the-unpronounceable-last-name, just what makes you think that you can work for me?"

As a rule Yohanna had a tendency toward modesty, but she had the distinct impression that the man interviewing her didn't value modesty. He valued confidence. She'd always had people skills, skills that allowed her to read others rather accurately. Lukkas Spader didn't strike her as a man who had the patience to work with meek people.

However she had a feeling that he respected—and expected—honesty. "Mrs. Parnell—"

He held up his hand, stopping her right there. "Who's Mrs. Parnell?"

"She's friends with Theresa Manetti, the woman who—"

He stopped her again. "I know who Theresa Manetti is," he told her. "Go on."

Yohanna picked up the thread exactly where she had dropped it. "She said you needed someone to organize your schedules, your notes and keep up to the minute on all the details of your projects."

He studied her for a long moment. She couldn't glean anything from his solemn, thoughtful expression. "And that would be you?" he finally asked.

Yohanna detected neither amusement nor skepticism in his voice. He was harder to gauge than most. Not to mention that the man was definitely making her nervous. Not because he was so good-looking but because she really wanted to get this job. She wasn't good at doing nothing.

Yohanna pulled herself together. She was determined not to let the producer see how nervous he made her. His world was undoubtedly filled with people who fawned over him. She wanted him to view her as an asset, not just another fawning groupie or "yes" person.

"That would be me," she replied, silently congratulating herself for not letting her voice quiver as she said the words.

The next moment she was relieved to see a smile playing on the producer's lips. The fact that the smile also managed to make him almost impossibly handsome was something she tried *not* to notice.

It was like trying not to notice the sun.

"You're pretty sure of yourself, aren't you?" he asked, amusement curving the corners of his mouth.

Yohanna raised her chin ever so slightly, an automatic reaction when she felt she was being challenged. "I know my strengths," she replied.

"Apparently so does Mrs. Manetti," he told her. "When we spoke, she spoke very highly of your qualifications, and I respect her judgment."

He continued looking at her, as if trying to discern if she was as good as the older woman had led him to believe. The silence dragged on for a good several minutes.

Yohanna had met the woman he was referring to only briefly. They had exchanged a few words and the interview had been arranged. There had been no time for Mrs. Manetti to form an opinion about her abilities one way or another.

She could feel herself fidgeting inside, and her pulse rate began to accelerate. All she could think of was that she really needed this job. She'd only been out of work for a couple of days, but the thought of prolonged inactivity had her already climbing the proverbial walls. Not to mention that she had enough money in the bank to see her through approximately one month—one and a half if she gave up eating.

As a last resort she could always move in with her mother, but as far as she was concerned, living under a freeway overpass was preferable to that. Her mother had been decent enough when Yohanna was growing up, but in the past eight years, only two topics of conversation interested her: marriage and children, neither of which was anywhere in Yohanna's immediate future.

She was fairly confident that living with her mother even for a day would swiftly become catastrophic.

Lukkas continued doling out information. "If you became my assistant, you'd be keeping irregular hours at best. I'm talking *really* irregular," he intoned, his eyes on hers. "And you'd be on call 24/7. Are you up for that?" he asked, looking at her intently.

"Absolutely," she assured him with as much confidence as she could muster.

But Lukkas still had his doubts. "You're not going to come to me in tears a week or two from now, saying that your husband is unhappy with the hours you're keeping and could I give you a more normal schedule, are you?"

"I don't have a husband, so that's not going to happen."

But Lukkas wasn't satisfied yet. "A fiancé? A boyfriend?"

"No and no," Yohanna responded, quietly shooting down each choice.

Lukkas still appeared skeptical. "Really? Not even a boyfriend?" His eyes never left hers, as if he considered himself to be an infallible human lie detector—and being as attractive as she was, the young woman couldn't possibly be telling the truth.

"Not even a boyfriend," she echoed, her face innocence personified.

"You're kidding, right?" he said in disbelief. How could someone who looked like this woman not have men lining up at her door, waiting for a chance just to spend some time with her? He knew this was none of his business or even ethical for him to ask, but curiosity urged him on.

"No," she replied. "I just never experienced that 'walking on air' feeling, si—Lukkas," she quickly corrected herself.

"Walking on air," he repeated. "Is that some sort of code?"

"More like a feeling," she explained then added quickly, "I've never met a man I felt I had chemistry with. In other words, I didn't experience any sparks flying between us. Without that, what's the point?" she asked with a vague shrug.

"What, indeed?" he murmured, thinking back, for a second, to his own solitary life. It hadn't always been that way.

Talking about herself always made her feel uncomfortable. Yohanna was quick to return to the salient point of all this. "The bottom line is that there isn't anyone to complain about my hours even if they do turn out to be extensive."

"No 'if' about it," he assured her. "They *will* be extensive. I'm afraid that it's the nature of the beast. I put in long hours and that means so will you." Again he peered closely at her face, as if he could read the answer—and if she was lying, he'd catch her in that, too. "You're all right with that?" he asked again.

"Completely."

"You haven't asked about a salary," he pointed out. The fact that she hadn't asked made him suspicious. Everyone always talked about money in his world. Why hadn't she?

"I'm sure you'll be fair," Yohanna replied.

Again he studied her for a long moment. He didn't find his answer. So he asked. "And what makes you so sure that I'll be 'fair'?"

"Your movies."

Lukkas's brow furrowed. He couldn't make heads or tails out of her answer. "You're going to have to explain that," he told her.

"Every movie you ever made was labeled a 'feel good' movie." As a child, the movies she found on the television set were her best friends. Both her parents led busy lives, so she would while away the hours by watching everything and anything that was playing on the TV. "If you had a dark side, or were underhanded, you couldn't make the kinds of movies that you do," she told him very simply.

"Maybe I just do it for the money." He threw that out, curious to see what she would make of his answer.

Yohanna shook her head. "You might have done that once or twice, possibly even three times, but not over and over again. Your sense of integrity wouldn't have allowed you to sell out. Especially since everyone holds you in such high regard."

Lukkas laughed shortly. "You did your research." He was impressed.

"It's all part of being an organizer," she told him. "That way, there are no surprises."

There were layers to this woman, he thought. "Is that what you consider yourself to be? An organizer?"

"In a word, yes," Yohanna replied.

He nodded, as if turning her answers over in his mind. "When can you start?"

There went her pulse again, Yohanna thought as it launched into double time. Was she actually *getting* the job?

"When would you want me to start working?" she

asked, tossing the ball back into his court. It was his call to make.

He laughed shortly. "Yesterday." That way, he wouldn't have lost a productive day.

"That I can't do," she told him as calmly as if they were talking about the weather. "But I can start now if you'd like," she offered.

Was she that desperate? he wondered. Or was there another reason for her eagerness to come to work for him? Since his meteoric rise to fame, he'd had friends disappoint him, trying to milk their relationship for perks and benefits. As for strangers, they often had their own agendas, and he had become very leery of people until they proved themselves in his estimation. That put him almost perpetually on his guard. It was a tiring situation.

"You can start tomorrow," Lukkas told her.

She wanted to hug him, but kept herself in check. She didn't want the man getting the wrong impression about her.

"Then, I have the job?" she asked, afraid of allowing herself to be elated yet having little choice in the matter.

"You can't start if you don't," he pointed out. "I'll take you on a three-month probationary basis," he informed her. "Which means that I can let you go for any reason if I'm not satisfied."

"Understood."

He peered at her face. "Is that acceptable to you?"

"Very much so, s-si—" She was about to address him as "sir" but stopped herself, uttering, instead, a hissing sound. "Lukkas," she injected at the last moment.

"I'm currently producing a Western. We're going to be going on location—Arizona. Tombstone area," he speci-fied. "Do you have any problem with that?"

She wanted to ask him why he thought she would, but this wasn't the time for those kinds of questions. They could wait until after she had entrenched herself into his life. The fact that she would do just that was a given as far as she was concerned now that he had hired her.

"None whatsoever," she told him.

"All right. Then go home and get a good night's sleep. I need you back here tomorrow morning at seven."

"Seven it is. I'll be bright eyed and bushy tailed," she responded, thinking of a phrase her grandfather used to use.

"I'll settle for your eyes being open," he told her. "See you tomorrow, Hanna."

Yohanna opened her mouth to correct him and then decided she rather liked the fact that her new boss was calling her by a nickname, even if she didn't care all that much for it. She took it as a sign they were on their way to forming a good working relationship.

After all, if someone didn't care for someone else, they weren't going to give them a nickname, right? At least, not one that could be viewed as cute. If anything, they'd use one that could be construed as insulting.

"See you tomorrow," she echoed. "I'll see myself out," she told him.

Lukkas didn't hear her, his mind already moving on to another topic.

Yohanna had to hold herself in check to keep from dancing all the way to the front door.

Chapter Two

The landline Yohanna had gotten installed mainly to placate her mother—"What if there's a storm that takes out the cell towers? How can anyone reach you then? How can *I* reach you then?"—was ringing when she let herself into her condo several hours later that day.

Yohanna's automatic reaction was to hurry over to the phone to answer it, but she stopped just short of lifting the receiver. The caller-ID program was malfunctioning, the screen only registering the words *incoming call*.

Frowning, she stood next to the coffee table in the living room and debated ignoring the call. Granted, everyone she knew did have this number as well as her cell number, but for the most part, if they called her, it was almost always on her cell phone, *not* her landline. *That* was for sales people, robo calls and her mother.

Which meant, by process of elimination, that the caller was probably her mother.

Yohanna was really tempted to let her answering machine pick up. Talking to her mother was usually exhausting.

But if she ignored this call, there would be others, most likely coming in at regular intervals until she finally picked up and answered. Her mother had absolutely unbelievable tenacity. She would continue calling, possibly well into the evening, at which time her mother would make the fifteen-mile trip and physically come over. Her hand would be splayed across her chest, as she would dramatically say something about her heart not being up to taking this sort of stress and worry.

Yohanna resigned herself to the fact that she might as well answer her phone and get the inevitable over with.

Taking a deep, bracing breath, she yanked the receiver from its cradle and placed it against her ear—praying for a wrong number.

"Hello?"

"It's about time you answered. Where were you? Never mind," Elizabeth Andrzejewski said dismissively. "I'm calling you to tell you that I've got your room all ready."

Yohanna closed her eyes, gathering together the strength she sensed she was going to need to get through this phone call.

Until just a minute ago she'd been walking on air, still extremely excited about being hired. She would have been relieved landing *any* job so quickly, on practically the heels of her recent layoff, but landing a job with Lukkas Spader, well, that was just the whip cream *and* the cherry on her sundae.

However, dealing with her mother always seemed to somehow diminish her triumphs and magnify everything that currently wasn't going well in her life. Her mother had a way of talking to her that made her feel as if she was a child again. A child incapable of doing anything right without her mother's help.

Yohanna knew that, deep down, her mother really meant well; she just wished the woman could mean well less often.

"Why would you do that, Mother?" she finally asked. She hadn't used her room since she'd left for college and moved out on her own.

"So you'll have somewhere to sleep, of course," her mother said impatiently.

"I *have* somewhere to sleep. I sleep in my bedroom, which is in my condo, Mother, remember?" Yohanna asked tactfully.

She heard her mother sigh deeply before the woman launched into her explanation.

"Well, now that you've lost your job, you're not going to be able to hang on to that overpriced apartment of yours. You should sell it now before the bank forecloses on it."

Yohanna was stunned. Where was all this coming from? She'd had this so-called "discussion" with her mother several years ago when she'd first bought her condo. Her mother couldn't understand why "a daughter of mine" would "waste" her money buying a "glorified apartment" when she had a perfectly good room right in her house. She'd thought that argument had finally been laid to rest.

Obviously she had thought wrong.

"The bank isn't going to foreclose on me, Mother," Yohanna informed her. "My mortgage payments are all up-to-date."

"Well, they won't be now that you've been fired," her mother predicted with a jarring certainty.

"Laid off, Mother," Yohanna corrected, trying not to grit her teeth. But there was no one who could make her crazier faster than her mother. "I wasn't fired, I was laid off."

"Whatever." The woman cavalierly dismissed the correction.

"There *is* a difference, Mother," Yohanna insisted. "One has to do with job performance. The other is a sad fact of modern life. In my case, it was the latter."

"Potato, po*tato*," her mother said in a singsong voice. "The bottom line at the end of the day is that you don't have a job."

The words suddenly hit her for the first time. "How did you find out?" Yohanna asked.

She hadn't told anyone about her layoff except for Mrs. Parnell, bless her. Granted, the people that she'd worked with knew, but a lot of them had been laid off, as well. She didn't see any of them sending her mother a news bulletin. They didn't even *know* her mother.

So how had her mother found out?

"I'm your mother," Elizabeth Andrzejewski replied proudly, as if that alone should have been enough of an explanation. "I know everything."

"You're not omnipotent, Mother," Yohanna told her mother wearily. "Spill it," she ordered. "Just how did you find out about the layoff?"

The silence on the other end of the line began to stretch out.

"Mother…" Yohanna began insistently.

Elizabeth huffed. "If you must know, I went to the office to surprise you and take you out for lunch today.

Imagine *my* surprise when I walked in and found out that you didn't work there anymore. Why didn't you tell me?" she asked, sounding as if she had been deeply wounded by this omission of information.

"I didn't want you to worry—or get upset," Yohanna answered.

That part was true, although there were many more reasons than that why she had kept the news to herself. Specifically, she didn't want to have to fend off her mother's offers for "help," all of which revolved around getting her to move back home. She'd moved out once, but she had a feeling that next time would be a great deal more difficult.

"You didn't want me to worry." Elizabeth practically sneered at the words. "I'm your mother. It's my job to worry about you. Now, I won't take no for an answer. I'll come over tomorrow morning to help you pack up your things and—"

Her mother was more relentless than a class-five hurricane, Yohanna thought. But she was not about to throw up her hands and surrender.

"I'm not selling the condo, Mother," she began patiently.

"All right, rent it out, then," her mother advised, frustrated. "That'll help you cover the cost of the exorbitant mortgage until you're about to get back on your feet again—"

"Mother, I *am* on my feet."

She heard her mother sigh again. This time, instead of sounding dramatic, there was pity in her mother's voice.

Irritating pity.

"There's no need to put up a brave front, Yohanna. Lots of people lose their jobs these days. Of course, if you had married Alicia Connolly's son, that nice young doctor, you wouldn't be in this predicament, wondering where your next dollar is coming from."

Her mother was referring to a setup she'd had her hand in. As Yohanna recalled the entire excruciating event, it had truly been the blind date from hell as well as ultimately being the reason she had vowed to *never* allow her mother to set her up with a date again.

"For your information, Mother," she said, enunciating each word so that her mother would absorb them, "I am *not* wondering where my next dollar is coming from."

"Well, then, you should be," Elizabeth told her with more than a touch of indignation in her voice. "The bank isn't going to let you slide because of your good looks, which, as you know, you're not going to have forever," she added, unable, apparently, to keep from twisting the knife a little bit. "Which reminds me. My friend Sheila has this nephew—"

Although she was always somewhat reluctant to keep her mother in the loop—mainly because her mother always found something negative to say about the situation—Yohanna knew that the older woman was not about to stop trying to manipulate her life—big-time—unless she told her mother that she was once again gainfully employed.

"Mother, stop, please," she pleaded. "I don't need to move back into my room or to rent out my condo."

"Oh, then, just what is your brilliant solution to your present problem?" Elizabeth asked.

I'm talking to my present problem, Yohanna thought.

However, she kept that to herself, knowing that if she ever said those words or similar ones out loud, her mother would be beyond hurt. She couldn't do that to the woman no matter how much her mother drove her up a wall.

"I've got a job, Mother," she told her.

"Honey, I told you that you don't need to pretend with me." It was obvious by her tone of voice that her mother simply didn't believe her.

"I'm not pretending, Mother," Yohanna answered, struggling to remain calm and clinging to what was left of her dwindling patience.

"All right." She could all but see her mother crossing her arms in front of her, fully prepared to sit in judgment. "And just what is this 'job' you've gotten so suddenly?" Before she could tell her, Yohanna heard her mother suddenly suck in her breath. "You're not doing anything immoral or illegal, are you?"

It was more of an accusation than a question. Among other things, her mother, an avid—bordering on rabid— soap opera fan, had a way of allowing her imagination to run away with her along the same creative lines that many of the soap operas she viewed went.

"No, Mother. Nothing illegal or immoral." She really hadn't wanted to tell her mother until her three-month probationary period was up, but, as with so many other things that involved her mother, she found that she had no choice in the matter. "I'm going to be Lukkas Spader's assistant."

"And just what does this man want being assisted?" Elizabeth asked suspiciously.

"Lukkas Spader, Mother," Yohanna repeated, stunned that her mother didn't recognize the name. "The *producer*," she added. But there was apparently still no recognition on her mother's part. "You know, the man who produced *Forever Yours*, *Molly's Man*, *Dangerous*." She rattled off the first movies that she could think of.

"Wait, you're working for *that* Lukkas Spader?" her mother asked, sounding somewhat incredulous.

Finally! Yohanna thought. "That's what I'm trying to tell you."

Suspicion leeched back into Elizabeth's voice. "Since when?"

"Since this morning, Mother, when Mr. Spader hired me."

Elizabeth obviously wasn't finished being skeptical about this new turn of events. "And what is it that you say you're going to be doing for him?"

Yohanna silently counted to ten in her mind before answering. "I'm going to be organizing things, Mother. Movie things," she elaborated, knowing how her mother tended to think the worst about every situation. Given the choice of picking the high road or the low one, her mother always went the low route.

As proved by her mother's next question. "Are you telling me the truth?"

Yohanna rolled her eyes. This was *not* a conversation that a thirty-year-old should be having with her mother. Anyone listening in would have thought her mother was talking to someone who was twelve. Maybe younger.

"Of course I'm telling you the truth, Mother."

To her surprise, instead of continuing to harp on the subject, she heard her mother give a huge sigh of relief. "Oh, thank God. Now, remember not to mess anything up, understand?"

"I'm not going to mess anything up, Mother." And then it hit her. She knew what her mother was think- ing. Yohanna nearly groaned. Her mother *never* gave it a rest. *Never.* "He's my boss, Mother," she said in a sharp warning voice.

"So?" Elizabeth asked defensively. "Bosses don't get married?"

Enough was enough. She was *not* having this conversation. "I've got to go, Mother. I've got some things to take care of before I go in tomorrow." It was a lie, but it was better than slamming the receiver down in the cradle, which she was very tempted to do.

Rather than attempt to pump her for more information, her mother surprised her by saying, "Go get some new clothes. Sexy ones. These Hollywood types like sexy women."

There was no point in arguing about this with her mother any longer. She had never known her mother to admit she was wrong or that she had overstepped her boundaries. Not even once.

There was no reason for her to hope that her mother would suddenly come to her senses at fifty-seven and turn over a new leaf.

For better or worse, this was her mother.

"Yes, Mother," Yohanna replied in a near-to-singsong voice. "Bye." And with that, she hung up, promising herself to get a new phone—one with a working caller ID—the first opportunity she got.

Yohanna didn't remember when she finally closed her eyes and fell asleep.

All she knew was that it felt as if she'd only been asleep for ten minutes before she opened her eyes again and saw that, according to the clock on her nightstand, it was quarter to six.

Spader wanted her at his Newport Beach home by seven.

Stifling a groan, she stumbled out of bed, then somehow made her way down the stairs and into the recently remodeled kitchen.

If she was going to get anything accomplished, she needed coffee. Deep, hearty, black coffee. Downing one cup fortified her enough to go back upstairs, take a shower and get dressed. All of which she did at very close to top speed. She needed to get out and on the road as quickly as possible.

She didn't anticipate any large traffic snarls from her home to Spader's but there was always a chance of a collision and/or a pileup—and she didn't like leaving *anything* to chance.

She also didn't like calculating everything down to the last possible moment. On time wasn't her style— being early was.

Fueled by an enormous amount of nervous energy, Yohanna was on the road less than half an hour after she'd woken up.

Twenty minutes after that, she was parked across the street from Spader's impressive three-story house. As usual, she was early and, ordinarily, she would walk up to the front door and ring the bell. She just assumed that to most people, being early was a plus. But Lukkas Spader might be one of those people who actually didn't like anyone arriving early, possibly before he was ready to see them.

She needed to find that little detail out before tomorrow morning. In the meantime, she looked at her wristwatch and continued to wait, parked directly across from his slightly winding driveway.

Which was where the patrol officer who tapped on her driver's-side window found her.

Startled by the knock—her mind was elsewhere— Yohanna looked up at the officer. To say she was surprised to see him was putting it mildly.

The officer motioned for her to roll down her window. Which, after one false start, she did.

"Is there something wrong, Officer?" she asked him, even though, for the life of her, she couldn't imagine what that could be, or why he'd want to speak to her in the first place.

"You tell me," he replied, waiting. When she continued watching him without saying a word in response to his flippant remark, the officer appeared to be losing patience as he asked, "Mind telling me what you're doing sitting out here all alone like this?"

"I'm waiting until seven o'clock," she explained. To her, it was all very logical.

"What happens then?" he asked.

She found the officer's tone just slightly belligerent, but told herself it was her imagination. "I knock on Mr. Spader's door."

The officer didn't seem to believe her. "And then what?" he demanded.

"He lets me in." Why was he asking all this? she wondered. She certainly didn't look unsavory.

"That the plan?" the officer said sarcastically.

Yohanna began to feel a little uneasy. "I don't think I understand."

The officer blew out a breath, sounding as if he was struggling to keep from raising his voice. "Look, honey, why don't you just drive off, buy yourself some popcorn and watch one of the guy's movies like everyone else does?"

The officer clearly didn't understand. "But Mr. Spader is waiting to see me."

"Sure he is," the officer said in a humoring voice. "You look like a decent kid. Stalking never ends well. Not for the stalker, not for the person they're stalking. So why don't you just—"

"Wait, what?" Yohanna cried, stunned at the very suggestion the officer was making. "I'm not stalking Mr. Spader," she insisted. "I work for him."

"Suuure you do." He stretched out the word, mocking her before he suddenly became stone-cold serious. "I don't want to take you in, but you're really not leaving me much of a choice here, lady. Now, for the last time, start your car and go home—"

"Ask him," Yohanna cried quickly. "He'll tell you that I work for him. Just go up to his door and knock." She was almost pleading now.

If she didn't show up the first day, she might as well kiss the job goodbye. And even if she wound up having the policeman escort her to Spader's door, the producer still might hand her her walking papers. No one wanted to knowingly work around trouble.

"You'd like that, wouldn't you? So you could tell all your little crazy loser friends that you got to see Lukkas Spader up close and personal-like. Sorry, I'm not in the business of making your pathetic little fantasies come true. Now, this is your last chance to go free—" he began again.

"Please, I'm telling you the truth, Officer. I work for Lukkas Spader. He told me to meet him here at seven this morning and I was just waiting until seven before knocking on his door. I am *not* stalking him," she insisted.

Still apparently unconvinced, the police officer frowned.

"You're not leaving me any choice. I warned you." One hand was now covering the hilt of his service weapon, ready to draw it out at less than a heartbeat's notice. "Get out of the car. Now."

One look into the man's eyes and Yohanna knew the officer wouldn't stand for being crossed. He wasn't the type to suffer any sort of acts of disobedience quietly or tranquilly.

Keeping her hands out where he could see them, Yohanna did as the police officer ordered. She got out of the car slowly.

"Is there a problem, Officer?"

The question came from someone standing directly behind the officer. Yohanna leaned over slightly to look, praying she was right.

She was.

It was Lukkas.

Yohanna's heart went into overdrive.

"No, sir, Mr. Spader. I just caught another stalker. This one's not as intense as the other one was, but she looks like trouble all the same."

Lukkas smiled as he stepped to the officer's side and looked at her. "She does, doesn't she?"

Chapter Three

"Do you want to press charges?" the police officer asked, looking expectantly at the man standing next to him.

Stunned, Yohanna's eyes widened considerably as she stared at the man she had *thought* was her new employer. Had her signals gotten somehow crossed and she'd misunderstood him yesterday?

No, that wasn't possible. He hadn't given her anything in writing, but she remembered every word he'd said and could recite them back to him verbatim. Her very precise photographic memory was part of what made her so good at organizing things. It also helped her take care of what needed to be done—and then remembering where everything was hours, even days, later.

She was about to nudge the producer's memory a little so this officer could move along when she heard Spader tell the man, "No, not at this time, Officer."

The police officer was still eyeing her as if she was some sort of a criminal deviant. She needed her new boss to say something a little more in her defense than a barely negligible remark.

"Mr. Spader, tell him I work for you," she requested with more than a little urgency.

The corners of Lukkas's mouth curved just a hint as he turned toward the officer and said, "She does, actually. This is Hanna's first day. She's here a little early," he commented. "But that's a good thing."

The officer removed his hand from his weapon. "Oh." There was just a sliver of disappointment in the man's voice. He glanced from the producer to the woman who had almost been arrested. "Sorry about that, but it's better to be careful than let things ride and then be sorry."

The apology was halfhearted, but Yohanna considered it better than nothing. She inclined her head, silently indicating that she accepted the officer's rather paltry excuse.

A huge range of emotions swirled through her like the wind gearing up before a storm. This was a whole different world that she was signing on for.

She focused on the one piece of information she had picked up out of all this. "You had a stalker?" she asked Lukkas incredulously. She'd occasionally read about things like that happening, both to famous celebrities as well as to average, everyday people, but it had never touched her life or happened to anyone she actually knew.

Until now.

"What happened?" she asked him.

Lukkas didn't answer her and gave no indication that

he had even heard her. Instead, what he said was, "Ready to get started?"

She took that to mean that the subject of his past stalker was off-limits. While her curiosity was still rather exceedingly ramped up, she could understand why the producer wouldn't want to pursue the subject. This was obviously something out of Spader's private life and she was just an employee—a *new* employee at that—hired on a probationary basis. That didn't exactly make her someone he was about to bare his soul to within the first few minutes of her first day on the job.

So she buried the question as well as her growing and somewhat unbridled curiosity and cheerfully replied, "Absolutely," to his question.

But even with her ready and eager to get started, it turned out that the producer wasn't quite ready to go back into his house just yet.

Instead, he took out what looked like a weather-beaten wallet from his back pocket. When he opened it, she realized that he wasn't holding a wallet. What Lukkas had in his hand was a checkbook.

The next moment he had turned toward the officer who was still standing there. "I heard that the department is collecting ticket money for their semi-annual basketball-for-charity game," Lukkas said as he began to write a more than substantial check to the Bedford Police Department, earmarking it for the basketball game.

Seeing the sum, the officer beamed, instantly forgetting all about the arrest he had been deprived of. "Yes, sir."

"Here." Lukkas tore out the check and handed it to the officer. "This might help a little."

Looking again at the sum the producer had written in,

the police officer's eyes seemed about to fall out of the man's head. Yohanna thought that perhaps the number hadn't quite registered when the man had first glanced at the check.

"Yes, sir, it sure would," the officer said with no small enthusiasm.

"Keep up the good work," Lukkas said, turning his back on the man and striding back to his house.

Yohanna tried to fall into place beside the producer. She found herself all but racing to keep up with him. In the background, she heard the patrol car driving away.

Glancing over his shoulder, Lukkas asked, "Am I walking too fast for you?"

"No," Yohanna answered stubbornly, doing her best to move even faster.

He stopped abruptly at his front door. Fueled by momentum, Yohanna almost crashed into him. Had he not caught hold of her shoulders just then, her body might have wound up vying for the exact same space that his was in.

Hiding his amusement, Lukkas held her in place for a moment. "Never be ashamed to admit the truth," he told her, referring to the answer she'd given him.

Rather than meekly accept the castigation, she lifted her chin ever so slightly and asked, "Does that work both ways?"

He didn't answer her immediately. He took his time, as if he was weighing something.

"Yes," he said after a beat.

She decided to see if he actually practiced what he preached. "Then, did you have a stalker?"

Releasing her shoulders, instead of being annoyed, Lukkas laughed. "Touché," he acknowledged, inclining his head.

Then he pulled open the front door. He'd left it un-locked earlier when he'd come out to see what was going on.

Yohanna just assumed the man was going to leave the question she'd repeated hanging in the air, unanswered. To her surprise, as she started to enter the house, she heard him say, "Yes, I had a stalker. It was a few years ago."

Closing the door behind them, Lukkas began to lead her through the house to the room he'd converted into his office. The same place where he had conducted her interview yesterday.

This time, since she was just a shade less nervous than she had been the day before, she took in more of her surroundings. Rather than modern or austere, the furnishings struck her as comfortable with warm, friendly lines. She wondered if her new boss had done the decorating himself, or if he had hired someone to do it for him.

Maybe he'd left it up to the woman she was replac-ing, she mused.

"Did they catch the person? The stalker," she clari-fied. Since Lukkas had opened up a little, she did her best to follow up on the subject. The more she knew about her employer, the more efficiently she could serve him.

"Why do you want to know?" As a rule, Lukkas didn't like being questioned. He turned the tables on his new assistant. Every word she uttered painted that much more of a complete picture of her.

"Just curious if there was still someone out there who felt they had the right to a piece of your life," she told him.

He thought that was rather a unique way of describing his stalker. Maybe there was more to this woman he'd hired than he'd thought, which was all to the good in his opinion.

"There's *always* someone out there, Hanna," he told her. "But if you're asking specifically if that misguided young woman is liable to pop up outside my window at a time of her choosing, the answer's no. To the best of my knowledge, she's still being treated as an inpatient at a psychiatric facility." This time he stopped right outside his office door. "Anything else?"

She got the distinct impression that the topic of conversation was to end right here, at his door. She wasn't quite sure if that meant she had stepped over some invisible boundary, or if the tone of voice he was using was just the way he sounded when he spoke to someone who was working for him.

If he decided to keep her on, she supposed she'd find out.

"Yes," she replied.

"Go ahead." There was no indication that he was running out of patience as far as she could see—which was good.

"Shouldn't I have filled out some sort of paperwork for your human resources department?" Yohanna asked.

Although overjoyed to actually be working, especially for someone like Lukkas Spader, there was still a small part of her that was highly skeptical about the validity of the entire arrangement. That left her wondering if perhaps, at the end of the day, she was not only off the record but completely off *any* books, as well.

Lukkas made no answer.

Instead, he pushed open the door to his office and silently gestured toward his desk.

There, lying on the blotter, away from the rest of the disorganized array that covered more than seven-eighths of his desk, were several pristine white pages stacked one on top of the other.

Crossing over to his desk, Yohanna saw that they appeared to be meant for her. Her first name was written on the top sheet.

"I would have put down your full name," he told her. "But there's no way in hell I would have spelled it right."

She smiled at that. Her last name had been misspelled more times than she could count.

"It took me two days to learn how to spell it when I was a kid. I thought about having it legally changed a couple of times," she confided, even though she had never gone through with it.

"Don't," he told her. "It has character. This is a place that tends to spew out carbon copies," he said, referring to his industry. "Being unique is a good thing." He paused for a moment. "When you finish with those, I'll give you a number and you can fax them to Human Resources," he told her. "Then we'll get down to the real work."

Yohanna had already sat down and begun filling out the employment forms.

Lukkas looked up from the preproduction notes he'd been working on. The center of his back was aching, the way it did when he remained immobile for a long period of time. It was due to an old college football injury, reminding him that he wasn't a kid anymore. He didn't like being reminded.

He glanced at his watch.

It was past seven-thirty in the evening. More than

twelve hours since he'd gotten started. Not that that was unusual. He was used to driving himself relentlessly whenever he was working on a project, especially at the very beginning of it.

He was also used to his people wearing out and leaving before his own day ended.

He had to admit he was surprised that this new woman not only hadn't said anything about the amount of time that had passed since she'd arrived at his house, but she appeared to be keeping up with the grueling pace he had set for himself.

Empty cardboard containers were piled up in the wastepaper basket beside his desk, evidence of the food they'd consumed. He'd sent out for lunch, but that had been close to six hours ago.

He felt his own stomach tightening in complaint, and he was accustomed to this sort of pace. He expected to hear Hanna's stomach rumbling at any second. He had no doubts that the woman probably thought he was some sort of an inhumane slave driver.

Pausing, he studied her unabashedly. She seemed to be oblivious to it, but that was probably an act. She didn't strike him as the type to be oblivious to *anything* in her immediate surroundings.

"You tired?" he asked her.

"No," she answered as she went over the notes he had completed earlier and handed to her. He'd wanted her to familiarize herself with what was involved on his end of preproduction. He planned to take her every step of the way just once. After that, she had to sink or swim on her own.

Raising her head for a split second to look in his direction, she assured him, "I'm fine."

"What did I say about the truth?" he asked her.

"Ah, a pop quiz. You didn't tell me about that." Her quick grin faded as she gave him the answer he required. "To never be afraid to admit it."

He nodded and then said, "Let's do this again. You tired?"

For a second Yohanna debated repeating her denial, but obviously that wasn't what Spader wanted to hear from her.

"Maybe a little," she allowed, even though it was against her nature to complain.

When he kept on looking at her, as if his eyes were drilling right into her mind, searching for the truth, Yohanna mentally threw up her hands and said, "Exhausted, actually."

The smallest of smiles briefly made an appearance on his lips. "There, that wasn't really so hard, was it?" he asked.

"It wasn't actually easy, either," she told him. "Especially since I wasn't sure what it was you wanted to hear," she admitted.

"The truth, Hanna, always the truth," he stressed. He put his pen down. Right now, this was more important than the notes he was making. "You're not going to do me any good if I have to read between the lines anytime I ask you a simple question. I need total honesty from you," Lukkas told her.

She spoke before she could censor herself. "No one wants total honesty. They just want *their* version of total honesty."

The words surprised him and managed to catch him completely off guard. He scrutinized her for a long moment, as if trying to decide something. "How old are you, Hanna?" he finally asked.

"Thirty."

He noticed there wasn't any hesitation before she volunteered the number. Most women over the age of twenty were coy when it came to the age question. She really was unique, he thought.

"Thirty, and already so cynical," he commented.

But Yohanna had a different opinion about her view. "Not cynical," she contradicted. "Being completely honest a hundred percent of the time is really cold and unfeeling."

He leaned back in his chair, rocking slightly as he regarded her. "How do you figure that?"

"For instance, if a girlfriend asks you if what she has on makes her look fat, she really doesn't want to know that she looks fat. What she really wants is to hear how flattering the outfit she's wearing looks on her."

"But if it really does make her look fat?" Lukkas asked, curious as to what her thought process was. "Aren't you doing that friend a disservice by *not* telling her the truth?"

Yohanna shook her head. "If it really does look bad on her, she'll figure it out on her own. She wants to hear flattering words from you."

"You can't be serious," he protested.

"Completely," she insisted. "What your friend will come away with is that you cared more about her feelings than making some kind of point by being a champion of the truth."

"In other words, you're saying it's all right to lie," he surmised.

"If you can't bring yourself to tell her a little white lie, say something nice about the color. Maybe it brings out her eyes, or makes her skin tones come alive."

"In other words, say anything but the word *fat*," he concluded.

She nodded. The smile began in her eyes and worked its way to her lips in less than a second. He found himself being rather taken with that. "*Fat* only belongs in front of the word *paycheck* or *rain cloud*."

"That's two words," Lukkas pointed out, not bothering to hide his amusement.

Yohanna suddenly became aware that she had been going on and on. Her demeanor shifted abruptly. "Sorry, I talk too much."

"You do," he conceded. "But lucky for me, so far it's been entertaining." Lukkas grinned, then after a beat, asked, "How's that?"

She wasn't sure what he was asking her about. "Excuse me?"

"I just threw in the truth, but then said something to soften the blow. I was just asking how you thought I did, if I got the gist of your little theory."

For a moment, as her eyes met his, Yohanna didn't say anything.

Was he being sarcastic?

Somehow, she didn't think so, but that was just a gut reaction. After all, she didn't really know the man, didn't know anything about him other than the information she'd gleaned from a handful of interviews she'd looked up and read yesterday before she'd come in for the interview.

Taking a chance that the producer was really being on the level, she smiled and said, "Very good," commenting on his "behavior."

"I wasn't trying to lecture you, you know," she told him in case he'd gotten the wrong impression. "I was just putting my opinion out there." And then she shrugged somewhat self-consciously. "My mother says I do that too much."

He instantly endeared himself to her by saying, "Your mother's wrong." She had to really concentrate to hear what he had to say after that. "There's nothing wrong with offering an opinion—unless, of course, you're delivering a scathing review on one of my movies. Then all bets are off."

"Has anyone ever done that?" she asked incredulously. Then, in case he didn't understand what she was asking, she repeated his words. "Given a scathing review about one of your movies?"

He didn't have to think hard. He remembered the movie, the reviewer, what the person had said and when. Why was it that the good reviews all faded into the background, but the one or two reviews that panned his movie felt as if they had been burned right into his heart?

"Once or twice," he answered, keeping his reply deliberately vague. The reviews hadn't exactly been scathing, but they had been far from good.

"Well, they were crazy," she pronounced. "You make wonderful movies."

He laughed at her extraserious expression. "You don't have to say that," he told her. "You already have the job."

"I'm not saying it because I want this job, I'm saying it because I really like your movies," she insisted. "They make me feel good."

"Well, that was their intention," he said, carrying the conversation far further than he had ever intended. He rarely discussed his movies this way. He spent a lot of time on the mechanics of the movie rather than the gut reaction to it. The latter was something he felt would take care of itself. It was just up to him to set the scene.

Chapter Four

"Do you get airsick?"

Lukkas's question came at her without warning.

As she had been doing for more than a week, Yohanna had driven to the producer's Newport Beach house.

She'd turned up bright and early, ready to put in another long day setting the man's professional life in order. He was bringing another project to life, and that involved an incredible amount of details that all needed to be attended to. Every day was a new learning experience for her.

She could hardly wait to get started every morning.

When she'd rung Lukkas's doorbell and he'd opened the door, she had offered up a cheerful, "Good morning."

Rather than return the greeting or say a simple hello, Lukkas had caught her off guard by asking if she'd ever experienced airsickness.

Stunned, Yohanna looked at him for a moment, then replied with a touch of vagueness, "Not that I know of. Why?"

"Good," he pronounced. "Because we're taking a little trip today."

She hung on to the word *little*.

"Anyplace in particular?" she asked when the producer didn't volunteer a destination.

He grinned in a way that made him almost impossibly sexy to her.

"Of course there's someplace in particular." He led the way back to his office. She saw his briefcase on his desk. It was open and he'd obviously been packing it when she'd rung the doorbell. "How many people you know fly around aimlessly?"

"Never conducted a survey on that." She watched him tuck a tablet into the briefcase, putting it between a sea of papers. "Do I get to ask where we're going?"

Lukkas paused, appearing as if he was trying to remember something. "You can always ask," he told her, sounding preoccupied.

"Let me rephrase that," she said out loud. "If I ask you where we're going, will you tell me?"

"I guess I'll have to." He closed his briefcase and flipped the locks into place. "Otherwise, it might be construed as kidnapping."

"As long as I'm on the clock, I don't think it can be called kidnapping." He walked out of his office. She fell into step beside him. "Not unless you tie me up," she put in as an afterthought.

The description made him laugh. Lukkas shook his head. "Did you talk like this at your last job?"

"Oddly enough," she answered, amused, "the topic of kidnapping never came up."

He speared her a long, penetrating look as he armed his security system and closed the door behind them. "So you didn't talk?"

"I didn't say that." She waited as he aimed the remote on his key chain at his car. All four locks flipped open. She got in on her side.

He tossed his briefcase onto the seat behind him, then got in behind the steering wheel. "You ever consider running for elective office? You've got all the evasion maneuvers down pat." Starting up his silver-blue BMW, he commented, "I'll say one thing about you. You've certainly got your wits about you. I like that."

She assumed that the first part of his comment was somehow tied to his query about whether or not she had any political aspirations. She couldn't think of anything she would have rather done *less* than that. Besides, the life she had jumped into, feetfirst, was getting more and more interesting by the minute.

"Then you won't mind telling me where we're flying off to." It wasn't a question but an assumption.

"Don't you like mysteries?" Lukkas asked, playing this out a little longer.

"Just to read, not when I'm in them," she told him honestly. "I like knowing. *Everything*," Yohanna elaborated.

"Does that mean you don't like surprises?" he asked.

Thinking of the way the so-called "layoff" had been sprung on her, there was only one way for her to answer that question. "Only for other people."

"A life without surprises." He rolled the idea over in his head as he squeaked through a yellow light that was already beginning to turn red. "Where's the fun in that?"

Lukkas spared her a quick glance. "You do like to have fun, don't you, Hanna?" he asked.

Finding herself being interviewed for a job by Lukkas Spader had been one giant surprise, but if she said so, he might mistakenly think she was flirting with him. There was no way she was going to allow her attraction to the man get in the way of her working for him.

"Lots of fun to be gotten without resorting to surprises," she pointed out.

On the freeway for all of four minutes, he took the off-ramp that promised to lead him to the airfield he needed.

"If you say so," he replied. "You like Arizona?"

Another question out of the blue. And then she remembered. He'd said something about his new project, a Western, being on location in Arizona. Was that where they were going?

Her stomach began to tighten up.

"I really can't say," she answered truthfully.

"And why is that?"

"I've never been to Arizona," she told him. He probably thought she was some sort of semirecluse. She hadn't been anywhere outside of a rather small area while he, she knew, was an international traveler, going wherever the movie took him.

"Well, Hanna, we are about to remedy that," Lukkas proclaimed.

Her eyes widened just a shade. "We're going to Arizona?" she asked, doing her best to hide her nervousness.

"That would be the natural assumption to make from what I'd just said, yes."

Traffic had gotten a little thicker. He was forced to go just at the speed limit rather than above it.

He hadn't mentioned anything about going on location to her yesterday. When had this happened?

"*Why* are we going to Arizona?"

"Because that's where the movie's going to be shot," he said, referring to his new "baby," a movie he had helped write, one based on his own story idea. "At least most of it. Whatever we can do indoors, we'll take care of at the studio. But there's no way, in this day and age, to be able to fake that kind of background—especially not Monument Valley," he added. He slanted a long look in her direction. "Ever hear of Monument Valley?" he asked.

So far, she seemed like efficiency personified, but that might be because she had him on the rebound from his previous relationship with Janice. He'd leaned on her completely. When she'd told him she was leaving, he'd felt as if his entire foundation was about to crack and dissolve into pieces under his feet.

Hanna had appeared just in time to be his superglue.

"Several of John Wayne's movies were shot there," she told him without pausing to think.

He smiled, impressed she knew that. Impressed with her. Something that was beginning to occur on a daily basis.

"You knew that," he said, somewhat marveled.

"I knew that," she reaffirmed. "So you're going to be shooting this film somewhere around—or in— Monument Valley?"

"No," he answered breezily.

Okay, now she was confused, Yohanna thought. "I don't understand. If you're not shooting there, why did you just ask me if I knew what Monument Valley was?"

"I thought I'd spring a pop quiz on you," he told her.

And then he grinned again. "And maybe Monument Valley will sneak in a time or two when we're shooting background shots for the movie. But right now we're going to be flying to Sugar Springs, Arizona. It's near Tombstone."

On what seemed like a winding road, they were approaching the small private airport that was his immediate destination. It housed approximately half a dozen private single-engine plans. Including his.

The area was a revelation to Yohanna. "I didn't know there was an airport there."

"There isn't," he told her, driving over to the hangar that housed his plane. "It's more like a landing strip than an airport. But the plane isn't very big, either, so it works out."

She looked at him, a queasiness beginning to work its way into the center of her stomach. "You can fly a plane, too?"

"I've got a few hours of piloting under my belt," he told her.

She immediately seized on what she hadn't heard. "But no pilot's license?"

"Not yet." He saw grave concern etching itself into her features. "Don't worry, I'm not the one who's going to be in the cockpit," he assured her. "I've got a pilot on call."

Lukkas was on the private airstrip now. He drove straight toward where his plane was waiting. Arrangements had been made with the pilot the night before. He'd wanted to make sure the plane would be gassed up, inspected and ready to fly by the time he arrived this morning.

"Your color's coming back," he informed her, amusement highlighting his tanned face.

She looked at him, bewildered. "Excuse me?"

"Just now, when you thought I was flying the plane, the color drained completely out of your face. It's back now," he noted.

"Must be the lighting in here," she said, grasping at any excuse. She didn't want him to feel undermined by what had to seem like a lack of faith in him. From what she'd learned, most of the producers had egos the size of Texas and wouldn't stand for any attempts at taking them down a peg or three.

Lukkas didn't appear to have an ego, but it was still too early in the game to tell.

"Maybe," he intoned, appearing to consider her comment about the lighting being responsible for her ghostly pallor a few minutes ago. "Contrary to what you might think, I don't have a death wish, and the only risk I take is when I cast certain performers thought to be washed up in the business by everybody and his brother. What they don't seem to understand," he continued, "is that if you show some faith in that person, they tend to try to live up to that image."

Parked now, he opened his door. "Let's go," he urged, getting out of his car. "Right now we're burning daylight."

He was already walking toward the airplane before she could say a word.

Yohanna wasn't exactly sure why he wanted her to accompany him on this flight. She'd effectively begun to organize his vastly overwhelming schedule so that he could actually have a prayer of staying on top of his agenda. Educating herself as best she could about the man she was taking all this on for, she'd begun to prioritize what absolutely needed to be done and what could wait for another day to come.

She had a feeling the reason Spader was so disorganized was that his mind raced around, taking everything he had to do into consideration, going first down one trail, then another and another. It seemed as though the man's day was filled with a great many starts and no conclusions. Without someone to take charge of the details and put them into a workable order, the producer was headed for a complete meltdown, which would in turn lead to utter chaos in his professional *and* his private life.

And she could do all that right from his office in Bedford. Which was why she didn't quite understand why he was taking her with him to Arizona. Especially when it all seemed rather spur-of-the-moment. At least, he hadn't mentioned anything to her about it yesterday.

"And why are we going there?" she asked.

"Let's call it a final run-through," he told her. "Among other things, I want to look around the town we're renting, make sure nothing modern's lying around to mess up a shot when we're filming. I don't want to be in post-production and suddenly looking at an iPod left on the bar or something equally as jarring."

Well, that part at least made sense. "And what am I going to be doing?" she asked.

"Off the top of my head, I'd say you can be the person taking notes to make sure that I can keep track of everything that occurs to me while I'm doing that run-through." Then he summed it up for her. "You'll do what every organizer does. You'll organize," Lukkas informed her.

Hurrying up the short portable stairs that had been

positioned beside the sleek plane, Lukkas greeted the pilot as he entered the plane.

"Jacob, this is Hanna Something-or-other. She'll be taking Janice's place," he told the pilot. "Hanna, this is Jacob Winter, the very best pilot around."

The pilot flashed a modest smile. "He's just saying that because I didn't crash the plane."

Obviously there was more to the story than just that, Yohanna thought, looking from one man to the other. But if there was, it would be a story for another day, she could tell.

Inclining his head ever so slightly for a moment, the pilot told Lukkas, "We'll be taking off as soon as you strap in."

Lukkas looked at her as if they were equal partners in this, not boss and employee. "Then, let's get strapped in."

A few minutes later Yohanna was gripping the armrests of her seat and holding her startled breath as she felt the single-engine plane begin its takeoff.

This was the easy part, she told herself, but she remained stubbornly unconvinced of this.

"I take it that you don't fly very much, do you?" Lukkas asked, looking at the way her very white knuckles seemed to protrude as Yohanna continued gripping the armrests.

"No," Yohanna answered without looking in his direction.

He thought he heard a slight quiver in her voice. That didn't seem like the young woman he was getting to know. "How often *have* you flown?" he asked.

This time she tried to turn her head to glance in his direction. But something seemed to almost hold her entire body in place. She recognized it as fear and started to mount a defense.

"Counting this time?" she finally responded, answering his question with a question.

"Yes."

She took in a shaky breath. "Once."

That would explain the white knuckles and the death grip she had on the armrests, Lukkas thought. "Then, why didn't you say something to me before we got on the plane?"

She forced herself to breathe normally. It was far from easy.

"Like what? Would you mind driving to this town I've never heard of in Arizona instead of flying? You're the boss," she pointed out. "That means that I'm supposed to accommodate you as best I can, not the other way around."

She kept impressing him when he least expected it. That went a long way in her favor. He'd begun to think that he could no longer be impressed by anything life had to offer. It was nice to know that he was wrong.

"I do like your work ethic, Hanna. This little arrangement just might work out after all." Glancing down at her hands, which were still wrapped around the armrests, gripping them for all she was worth, he told her, "I won't even charge you for having to replace the armrests."

She was acting like a child, not a grown woman, Yohanna upbraided herself. Though it took almost superhuman effort, she forced her hands to let go of the armrests, although it took her a while to get all ten fingers off at the same time.

"Sorry," she murmured.

"Nothing to be sorry about," Lukkas countered. "Lots of people have flying issues."

"You probably think I'm being childish. I mean, I know that the odds against the plane going down are really tremendously low and that, comparably, a lot more people die in car crashes than plane crashes, but what my brain knows and the rest of me knows hasn't become fully reconciled yet."

Yohanna took another long, steadying breath and then let it out slowly, growing just a shade more in control of herself as she did so.

That was when she noticed Lukkas's encouraging, amused smile had completely faded from his lips. It was replaced with a solemnity she hadn't witnessed on the man before.

Obviously something had suddenly changed.

Every single instinct she possessed told her that something was wrong, but as to what, she hadn't a sliver of a clue.

Since she had been the only one talking when this transformation had occurred for Lukkas, it had to be either something she'd said, or a thought that had unexpectedly crossed the man's mind.

If it was the latter, then she was at a total loss how to remedy that. She had no way of discovering what had occurred to him to make him turn one hundred and eighty degrees.

However, if it was something that she had inadvertently said, then the advantage was hers.

But what had she said that could have affected him this way? She'd just cited statistics between plane crashes and car crashes.

Replaying the past few minutes in her head, she decided that it couldn't have been anything to do with plane crashes because Lukkas had still been grinning after she'd mentioned them.

That left car crashes.

Someone he had known must have died in a car crash. The more she went over that abbreviated section of time in her head, the more certain she became that she was right in her estimation.

But there was no way she could just ask Lukkas about that outright. If nothing else, in the long run that would be like pouring salt into a freshly reopened wound just to satisfying her curiosity.

There had to be another way to find out if she was right.

She thought of Cecilia's friend, Mrs. Manetti, who had initially set up her interview with the producer. Mrs. Manetti might know.

And then, she thought as the silence between Lukkas and her continued, there might even be a faster way to find out if she hadn't stuck her fashionably shod high-heeled foot into her unsuspecting mouth.

Her hooded eyes watched Lukkas for any sign that he was about to turn to her or to say something. He seemed very preoccupied with whatever was in the black folder he kept within easy reach, at least from what she'd discerned so far. She quietly turned on her smartphone.

Still watching Lukkas, she pulled up a search engine and typed in the words *car accident* and then his name.

The signal reception was reduced to only two bars, rendering the search engine exceedingly sluggish. She watched the little circle that indicated the site was being loaded go around and around for so long, she felt it was stuck in this mode.

She was about to give up for now and close her phone when she saw the tiny screen in her hand struggle to stabilize both two photographs and the words written directly beneath them.

She'd assumed that the words would become clear first, but it was the photographs—a beautiful young woman in one and a car that looked as if it had been turned into an accordion in the other—that materialized several minutes before the words.

After an eternity the circle stopped swirling and disappeared, leaving in its wake the headline from a newspaper article: Producer's Pregnant Wife Killed in Car Crash.

The article identified the dead woman's husband as Lukkas Spader.

Chapter Five

Stunned and appalled, Yohanna could only numbly stare at the heart-wrenching headline, unaware that her mouth had literally dropped open.

The next moment her brain kicked in and she quickly pressed the home button at the bottom of her smartphone. An array of apps sprang up, very effectively replacing the article as if it had never been there to begin with. Under different circumstances, she would have gone on to read the article, but this was definitely not the time for her to fill in the gaps.

The idea of Lukkas looking over and accidentally seeing what she was reading was just unthinkable to her. It was bad enough that she'd carelessly said what she'd said just now, comparing the crash rate of planes to cars. It didn't matter that she hadn't known Lukkas's wife had lost her life in an event that she had so cavalierly tossed out. Her not knowing hadn't lessened the pain Lukkas undoubtedly felt at the unintentional reminder of his loss.

More than anything, she would have loved to apologize to him, to tell him that she hadn't known he'd lost his wife this way. Until just now, she hadn't thought that he was ever married.

She'd done her homework on him but only partially so. To do her job well, she had been trying to educate herself about Lukkas Spader the producer, not the private man. The one article that had touched on both his professional *and* his private life had referred to him as being one of Hollywood's most eligible bachelors. That, to her, had translated to his not being married.

Had the article been written by a more accurate writer, it would have made some sort of a reference to his being a widower. At least that would have given her some sort of a heads-up.

Yohanna slanted a look in his direction. How did she go about making this right? She didn't have a clue, so for now, all she could do was leave the matter alone.

"We're about to land," Lukkas told her, his deep voice cutting through the fog still swirling around her head. "You might want to secure that." He nodded at the smartphone still in her hand.

"Yes, of course." Feeling like someone who was just now coming to, Yohanna quickly slipped the device back into her pocket.

After a beat, as they began their slow descent, Lukkas quietly said, "They said that she didn't feel any pain."

Yohanna's head jerked up as she looked at him. Had Lukkas glimpsed the article she had pulled up on her phone? She fervently hoped not.

But then, how did she explain the remark he had just made?

"Excuse me?" she said in the most innocent voice she could muster.

"My wife. Her car crash," Lukkas said, filling in the pertinent words. "The first responders on the scene said she died instantly and mercifully hadn't felt any pain. She didn't even have time to react, actually." Then, as if aware that he was speaking in fragments, he told her, "I saw you looking up the article."

There was no point in trying to deny it, Yohanna thought. She wasn't about to insult him like that or by pretending that he could be diverted by some fancy verbal tap dancing. He'd already showed her that he valued honesty.

"I'm so sorry, I didn't know. I wouldn't have made that thoughtless comparison about planes and cars if I had known about your wife."

"I know," Lukkas told her. An extremely bittersweet smile curved just the edges of his mouth. "It's just that, even after almost three years, I'm still not really used to it." His voice took on a wistful tone. "There are times that I still expect to hear her voice, or see her coming out of the kitchen, telling me she's in the mood for pizza when what was really going on was that she'd burned dinner beyond any hope of recognition—again," he added, grinning as he fondly recalled the memory.

"I am so very, very sorry," she told the producer in what amounted to a whisper.

Yohanna felt utterly helpless. She wasn't going to mouth the utterly overused and hopelessly clichéd phrase that she was sorry for his loss because it didn't begin to encompass, in her opinion, the grief the man must have felt and that he still continued to feel.

She remembered when her father had died the summer that she'd turned twelve; for weeks afterward she just couldn't find a place for herself. It was as if every place, both physically and emotionally, felt wrong to her, as if she didn't belong in it. It didn't matter if that place was familiar to her or not, she was still uncomfortable.

It had taken her a long time to make peace with her sense of loss. She couldn't begin to imagine what it must have been like for Lukkas to lose a spouse, not to mention their unborn child, as well.

"Yeah, me, too," Lukkas murmured more to himself than to her.

The next moment she saw the producer unbuckling his seat belt.

"Wait, shouldn't you keep that on?" she asked, afraid her initial careless observation had triggered a reckless reaction from Lukkas.

"Only if I want to try to take this chair with me on location." He pointed to the window next to her. "We've landed."

She blinked and looked out. They were on the ground. How had that happened without her realizing it?

"Oh."

She felt foolish. So far, today wasn't going well *at all*. She'd been so concerned about his feelings of loss as well as how callous he must have thought she'd sounded that she hadn't even paid attention to the fact that the plane had descended and made its landing.

Lukkas pulled down his briefcase from the overhead compartment. "Don't worry, you'll be a seasoned flier in no time," he assured her, verbally moving on and putting a world of distance between himself and the previous topic.

Unbuckling, Yohanna grabbed her things and was on her feet, following him off the plane. As she went, she made a mental note to find the article again when she got home tonight. She wanted to familiarize herself with the details of the story so she wouldn't be guilty of making another thoughtless reference to a very painful period in his life.

The sun, definitely not in hiding when they left Bedford, seemed to have been turned up to High as it greeted her the second she left the shelter of the single-engine Learjet. She shaded her eyes with her free hand, but that still didn't make visibility even an iota more tolerable.

Halfway down the ramp that had been placed beside the plane's open door, Lukkas turned toward her. "Watch your step," he warned. "The sun can be a little blinding out here until you get used to it."

She had a habit of dashing up and down the stairs without bothering to even marginally hold on to any banister or railing. But because Lukkas had specifically cautioned her, she thought it best to slip her hand over the railing and slide her palm down along the bar as she descended. She didn't want him to think that she was ignoring his advice.

Besides, it never hurt anything to be careful—just in case.

There was a silver-green, fully loaded Toyota waiting for them. It was parked well inside the gates. The plane hadn't landed far from it.

"Welcome back, Mr. Spader," the man standing beside the vehicle called out to Lukkas the second they were within hearing range. Of average height and build, looking to be around forty or so, with a thick, black head of hair, the man opened the rear door behind the driver's side, then waited until they reached the vehicle.

"Thanks for coming to pick us up, Juan," Lukkas said to the driver. Then he nodded in her direction. "This is Hanna. She'll be taking Janice's place."

The man he had called Juan nodded at her politely, then flashed an easy smile. "You've got your work cut out for you, Hanna," he told her. "Janice found a way to be everywhere at once."

No pressure here, Yohanna thought. She forced a smile to her lips in response. "I'll give it my best shot."

Lukkas spared her a look before he gestured for her to get into the vehicle first. "You'll have to do better than that to stay on the team," he informed her. "I can't have you just trying, I need you *doing*." He pointedly emphasized the word.

Really no pressure here, Yohanna thought, feeling a little uneasy—but just for a moment. The thing about pressure was that feeling it made her more determined than ever to succeed. She had decided a long time ago to be one of those people who had made up her mind to rise to the occasion rather than to fold under the specter of insurmountable obstacles or to listen to someone when they said something couldn't be done.

She was, at bottom, a doer. It wasn't in her nature not to give something her absolute all.

"Don't worry about me. With all due respect to Janice, I'll do whatever you need done," she replied with quiet determination. "And I'll do it fast."

Listening—even though he looked to be elsewhere—Lukkas inclined his head, as if conducting a conversation with himself.

"We'll see," he said, and then repeated even more softly, "We'll see."

Yohanna squared her shoulders. *We sure will*, she silently promised.

"Did you do this?" she asked Lukkas, wonder clearly shimmering in her voice as, twenty minutes later, she stared at the town coming into view.

At first glance, it was as if all three of them—Lukkas, Juan and she—had crossed some sort of a time-travel portal, one that separated the present from the long-ago past.

Sitting inside a brand-new state-of-the-art vehicle, she found herself looking out at a town that for all the world appeared to have literally been lifted from the late 1800s. Here and there were horses tied to hitching posts outside weathered wooden buildings, the tallest of which was, very obviously, the town saloon. The streets were paved not with asphalt or cement but dirt—hard, sun-baked, parched, cracked dirt.

Rolling down the window on her side, Yohanna leaned out to get a better view. Everything that she would have imagined to have existed in a slightly romanticized version of the Old West seemed to be right here. She began taking inventory.

There was a newspaper office, a barbershop that doubled as a doctor's office, and an emporium that was twice as wide as the other buildings because it contained the only so-called shopping area for the citizens of and beyond the town.

There was another rather dilapidated tiny hole-in-the-wall building, which, she saw as they drew closer, was actually the sheriff's office. One street away, dominating almost that entire block and two stories tall, was the town's one and only saloon. Big and gaudy, the Birdcage Saloon seemed primed for business even at this early an hour in the morning.

"No." Lukkas answered her question. "I found the town like this. It's perfect, isn't it?" She didn't know if he was still talking to her or sharing something with someone in his mind. "Pull over here, Juan," he instructed, pointing.

"Here" was in front of the saloon. Getting out, he waited for her to slide out of the car after him.

When she did, Yohanna looked around in complete wonder, unable to make up her mind whether or not the producer was putting her on. While the town looked weathered, something about it didn't strike her as genuine.

She couldn't put her finger on it, but this old-fashioned Western town didn't appear 100 percent authentic to her, either.

"You didn't help it along to arrive at this Old West town look?" she asked.

She'd initially looked too innocent to be this sharp, he thought. He didn't know whether to be proud that she could be this forthright, or leery of dealing with her on general principle.

In either case, she was still waiting for an answer, he reminded himself.

"I didn't, but Jeff Richards did."

The name meant nothing to her. Yohanna shook her head. "I'm afraid I don't—"

He hadn't expected her to know who he was referring to unless she'd read the article in that popular magazine a few months ago.

"Richards is the one who bought this entire town by paying off its back taxes. It was his idea to turn it into a tourist attraction," he told her. "He was trying to make it into a Tombstone look-alike." He went on to explain. "We're renting it for the duration of filming the exterior shots—and a couple of the interior ones, as well. After that, we fold up our tents—or get into our trailers and drive as it were—and he gets his town back with the added benefit of being able to advertise that *The Sheriff From Nowhere* was filmed here on location."

He smiled to himself about the predictability of the situation. "You'd be surprised what a little publicity like that does to attract people. By the way, while we're renting this town, it'll be your job to make sure Richards gets his checks on a regular basis. You'll also make me aware of any snags, misunderstandings and problems that might crop up due to our arrangement."

"Problems?" she questioned.

"Like fees suddenly being raised or doubled. You'd be surprised what some people try to pull," Lukkas told her.

"Got it," she said, making a notation in her notebook.

That she had written down what he'd said caught his attention. "Why aren't you making an entry on your smartphone calendar?"

"I will," she told him, wondering if he thought she was archaic in her methods. "But I have to admit that I like the feel of putting a pen to paper when I make my notes. This way, I'll wind up with two sets of records about the things I'm supposed to take charge of and keep after."

Yohanna had a feeling this was going to be a lot to contend with, especially since she knew the man's actual handwriting looked to be about preschool level quality. It was difficult to make heads or tails out of some of it.

She would have preferred if he had dictated and recorded his notes into his cell phone. But although it was apparent he felt electronic devices were tremendous work savers, in the long run, he obviously still was very tied to the old-fashioned way of keeping track of the events—large and small—of his life.

"Huh," he murmured in response to her claim of liking the feel of putting pen to paper.

Lukkas couldn't help but wonder if she was being genuine, or if she was merely saying that because she'd learned from someone that he felt the same way about the notes he made to himself.

The veteran producer was the first to admit that he was scattered from here to eternity and the notes he cared about…well, they could still be found somewhere between those two points. He had good intentions, but heaven knew he wasn't organized.

That was where she was supposed to come in.

It was up to her to keep after him as well as to make his hectic world as organized as humanly possible.

"There's Dirk Montelle," Lukkas suddenly announced, giving the man the hello sign when the latter looked in their direction. "He's signed on to direct this little movie," he told her.

The man had a real gift for understatement, she thought. That was a revelation to her.

She would have thought that a man of his capabilities, not to mention the perks he probably had written into his contracts, would have had a giant ego and a way of pounding his own chest and putting everyone else down. She'd known men like that before. Actually *dated* men like that before she'd decided she was better off sitting home alone than being out with one of these egotists, chairing a fan club meeting of one.

But before she could make some sort of a response to his last comment, Lukkas was taking off, striding across the parched and cracked streets to reach the man he had ultimately selected to helm his movie. He'd told her how he'd thought long and hard over making an offer to the director. This was his life's blood up there. That was a hard thing to ignore or even remain neutral about. Finally getting the proposed movie off the storyboards and onto a set with a final script was like having a dream come true. The movie he was now in charge of making had been a secret project of his for the past ten years.

Watching Lukkas pick up his pace, Yohanna shook her head. She picked up her own pace to make up for the head start the man had on her. Yohanna pressed her lips together, looking for strength even though she knew it could have been so much worse.

Even so, she couldn't help wishing that Lukkas would give her some kind of a warning before he took off like that.

She assumed he wanted her to get acquainted with the people working on this film so that when he asked her to do something with one of the cast or crew, she would know who he was talking about.

That meant becoming familiar with the names and jobs of more than two hundred people.

Fast.

Well, she'd wanted something a little more exciting than the work she'd done before, right? Office manager for the law firm had been good, steady work—until it wasn't, of course, and she'd become a casualty of the company merger—but it had also admittedly been dull as dishwater in its day-to-day routine.

This, however, had the makings of some sort of a wild, no-holds-barred adventure in fantasyland. For the moment—and hopefully for some time to come if everything went well—she would be dealing with both the present-day world and the past, and probably the future if what she'd heard about the producer's next project was true.

The words *dull* and *boring* were definitely not words to be applied to this job description, Yohanna thought happily.

"C'mon, catch up, Hanna," Lukkas urged as he turned for a moment in her direction and called out to her. "We don't want this project to start falling behind schedule before it even gets under way."

"No, sir," she responded—only to have Lukkas shoot her a look that stopped her in her tracks.

Instantly she realized her mistake. "No, Lukkas," she corrected herself.

"Hope you learn the routine faster than you learned that," he commented.

"Old habits are hard to unlearn," she told him.

"Didn't ask for an explanation, Hanna," Lukkas pointed out. "Just make it happen, starting now."

She inclined her head rather than open her mouth. Just for now, Yohanna thought that it might be better that way.

Chapter Six

If Dirk Montelle had been cast in a movie, Yohanna thought as she quickly followed Lukkas and drew closer to the director, he would have played a college professor. Montelle looked the type—almost stereotypically so—right down to the pipe that she'd read was never out of arm's reach.

For the most part, the man didn't smoke it as much as he kept it around to chew on its stem. According to an interview he'd given recently, it helped him cope with the countless tensions and crises that went along with being in the business of making fantasies come to life for a brief amount of time.

The longtime veteran director paused for a moment, cutting short his exchange with the person he was talking to, to greet Lukkas. When his steel-gray eyes shifted over to look at her, the affable director grinned broadly and then shook his head, not in a negative way but in apparent admiration.

"So I see you already heard," the director said to Lukkas.

"Heard what?" Lukkas asked as he shook the man's hand.

"About our little crisis. She certainly is pretty enough," the man said appreciatively, taking full measure of Yohanna. "If she can sound believable saying her lines, she's in." Appearing exceedingly satisfied, the director put his hand out to her and introduced himself. "Dirk Montelle. And you are…?"

"Very confused," Yohanna confessed as she glanced from the enthusiastic director to her equally confused-looking boss.

At least it wasn't just her, Yohanna thought with relief.

"Montelle, what the hell are you talking about?" Lukkas asked.

The director's expressive eyebrows rose high on his wide forehead. "You mean you didn't bring her here to replace Monica Elliott?" he asked, referring to the actress playing one of the more prominent supporting roles.

"Why would I want to replace Monica Elliott? The woman's got the mouth of a sailor on shore leave after six months at sea, but the audiences still seem to love her. All her recent films have been hits," Lukkas reminded the director.

Although, in his personal opinion, the egotistical actress was skating on very thin ice and living on borrowed time. Any day now, he expected to see a news bulletin that the twenty-seven-year-old actress had crashed and burned.

"Yeah, well, they're going to have to love someone

else," Dirk told him. "She walked out yesterday, saying that she decided to honor the commitment she'd broken to be in our movie."

Lukkas looked at his director. "Monica had another commitment?" This was the first he was hearing about there being another movie, much less that the high-living actress had broken a contract to film his movie instead.

Dirk nodded. "She said that the first contract predates the one she has with us by fifteen days."

"And what made her suddenly change her mind to switch back?" Lukkas asked.

Dirk raised his wide shoulders in an exaggerated shrug then let them fall almost dramatically. "With her, who knows? Somebody said something about Monica being angry that Angelica Fargo had more lines than she did." The director sighed. "Bottom line is that we're down the second lead." He turned toward Yohanna. "Sure you don't want to give it a whirl?" he asked, sounding almost half serious. "You look about the same size as Monica, so Wardrobe wouldn't be unhappy."

Though flattered, Yohanna's thoughts were focused elsewhere. "Did you see it?" she asked.

Dirk looked at her uncertainly. He hadn't a clue what she was asking. "See what?"

"The other contract," Yohanna stressed. "Did you see the date on it?"

Lukkas realized what his assistant was getting at. "Well, did you?" he asked his director and old friend.

The expression on Dirk's face was that of a man wondering if he had been duped. "Actually, no. I took her word for it. She said something about her lawyer holding on to it. The threat she was silently issuing was that she'd sue and hold up production on the picture if we didn't let her out of this contract."

"What are you thinking?" Lukkas asked Yohanna.

"That she might be bluffing. I could be wrong, but judging by her recent actions—yes, I watch those tabloid programs—that might be something she'd be prone to do, lie to get out of a contract she decided wasn't to her advantage to honor for some reason. It should be an easy thing to check out."

Lukkas turned his attention to his director. "You know anyone on the other set? Someone who might be able to confirm—or dispute—when the contracts for all the major players were signed?"

Montelle suddenly looked very pleased with himself—and impressed with Lukkas's newest addition to his crew. "As a matter of fact, I know a few people."

"Knew there was a reason I hired you," Lukkas quipped. Then he looked at Yohanna. "Nice catch."

"*Possible* catch," she amended.

"Modest, too. Looks as though I got lucky. Remind me to throw some more business Mrs. Manetti's way," he told her. "And while you're at it, give Joanne Campbell's agent a call."

"The actress?" she asked a little uncertainly. Joanne and Monica looked alike enough to be sisters. Why would he need one if he was keeping the other?

"No, the librarian," he deadpanned. "Of course, the actress. The part's a good fit for her."

"But what about Monica?" Yohanna asked him. "Didn't you just say—?"

He held his hand up to keep her from going on. "I want to give her a hard time to show her that it's not good business to create her kind of turmoil on one of my sets. She made Montelle here sweat. Now it's our turn to make *her* sweat. Sound good to you?" he asked the director.

The man's grin said it all, but just in case, he confirmed, "Absolutely. Music to my ears, boss."

His attention back to the director, Lukkas told the man, "If you need me, I'll be in the trailer for a while—" He suddenly paused. "The trailers did arrive, right?"

"Yesterday," Montelle confirmed. "Most of them anyway. The rest are on their way. Should be here by the end of the week. What's a production without glitches?" the director asked.

"A production that doesn't have me eating migraine tablets by the pound," Lukkas responded.

Dirk snapped his fingers as if he'd had a life-altering idea.

"That's how I'll fund my retirement. I'll buy stock in your migraine medication," he said, almost succeeding in keeping a straight face.

"Coming?" Lukkas asked Yohanna after he began walking away.

There he went again. "Would you take offense if I had a bell collar make up for you?" she asked Lukkas, once again quickly striding after him to catch up.

"I don't wear jewelry," he responded, straight-faced.

"Don't think of it as jewelry," she told him. "Think of it as an early warning system. Kind of like with earthquakes."

Lukkas rolled her explanation over in his mind. "I think I like that comparison, but I'm not sure. Get back to me on that," he instructed.

"Right," she mumbled under her breath.

* * *

"This is your trailer?" Yohanna asked, clearly wowed as she walked into it.

He tossed the briefcase he'd brought with him onto the nearest flat surface. "Yes. Why?"

She suppressed a low whistle. "My first apartment was smaller than this. I think my second one was, too."

"Sorry to hear that," he said wryly. "This is my production headquarters when I'm away from the studio. I need the space to think. Small, tight places don't let me think."

"Whatever works," she said agreeably, still taking it all in.

"You can put your things down over there," Lukkas told her, pointing to what looked like a spacious alcove, complete with a compact acrylic desk and a landline.

The latter had her looking at him quizzically. She nodded at it, waiting for him to explain. Why a landline when the logical way to go would have been another cell phone?

"It's my tribute to my past," he told her. "I like blending old and new together. It does nobody any good to let old traditions die unnoticed and forgotten."

"Okaaay," she murmured, drawing out the word.

"And now," he told her, "on that note, I've got several phone calls to make—and if I'm not mistaken, you do, too."

"Right," she agreed, putting down the laptop that she'd packed this morning. Flipping it open, she began initializing her access to the internet.

"Of course I'm right," Lukkas quipped. "That's why they pay me the big bucks." His eyes narrowed just a touch as he looked at her. "That's a joke, Hanna."

Her mouth quirked a touch. "I knew that." Her eyes sparkled with a whimsical glimmer that he found rather compelling.

Perhaps just a little *too* compelling, he silently warned.

Taking a breath to fortify himself, Lukkas said, "Hard to tell at times," and then went off to the section of the custom-built trailer that doubled as a bedroom whenever he remained on a set overnight.

Yohanna found that working for Lukkas Spader on a movie set was a real learning experience. She discovered that while he was the producer on record, there were several positions that bore part of his title and were considered to be under his supervision.

There were assistant producers, coproducers and executive producers to name just a few, and none of them had the sort of responsibility and authority that Lukkas with his simpler title possessed.

She learned very quickly that he took his position quite seriously, relinquishing none of the myriad parts.

He had conceived of the idea for this movie, nurtured it along and then cowrote the script after having written the initial treatment. He'd been involved in the casting of the film, retaining his right of final veto if someone didn't strike him as being right for the part.

According to what she learned from one of the camera crew, Lukkas always took casting approval very seriously, right down to the extras who were to be used in several of the saloon scenes.

He also, the cameraman informed her, tended to use the same crew over and over again, shepherding them from one movie to another. They were, in effect, one large, mostly happy family.

"The man's as loyal as anyone you'll ever be lucky enough to know—pretty rare in this business, let me tell you," the veteran cameraman had rhapsodized.

"How many movies have you made with him?" she asked, curious.

"Five, counting this one," the man, Eddie, had answered as he continued setting up his equipment. "But there're guys here who've been with The Spade from the beginning. He once said that if he liked the quality of someone's work, he didn't see a reason why he shouldn't use that person again."

"Wait, 'The Spade'?" she questioned uncertainly. Were they still talking about Lukkas?

The man nodded. "That's what the crew calls him. Because of his last name," he added.

She had to admit that she wouldn't have thought of that herself. But now that the cameraman had pointed it out to her, she couldn't see how she could have missed that.

"He knows everyone's name. I really don't know how he keeps them all straight. Me, I've got five kids and sometimes I forget some of their names, or get who's who mixed up," he joked. "I never heard The Spade confuse anyone's name with someone else's. The guy's incredible."

There'd be no argument from her on that. But, admiration notwithstanding, she was starting to understand why the producer needed to have someone organizing things for him as he went along. It was apparent that he already had far too much going on in his head to accommodate anything extra.

In all honesty, she was beginning to wonder how the man didn't just implode—or have a meltdown. There was just too much.

* * *

"So how's it going?" Lukkas asked sometime later that day as he came up on her.

"I located Joanne Campbell. Her agent—Jim Myers—said she was in between projects at the moment and would love to have a chance to work with you. Seems you have quite a following," she told him with a smile.

She had to confess that she felt a touch of pride about the matter as well, which she supposed anyone else would have thought somewhat premature. But in all honesty, she was beginning to feel as if she had always had this job. To his credit, Lukkas created that sort of atmosphere on his sets.

Lukkas was quick to wave away the comment she had repeated. "Her agent knows how to sugarcoat his words, that's all. Helps during negotiations."

"Myers wanted to know when you'd like to have Joanne audition for the part."

"No need," Lukkas told her. "She's already got the part." When Yohanna looked at him in surprise, he explained his reasoning. "She has the same build, the same coloring as the Elliott girl and—as a plus—she has a hell of a better attitude than Monica Elliott does." Lukkas had few hard and fast rules on his set, but Monica Elliott had broken one of them. "I don't like turmoil on my sets."

"Turmoil," Yohanna echoed. "I don't see how that's even possible, considering the size of the fan club you've got here." She'd initially decided to keep that to herself, but when something was staring you in the face, there was a tendency to want to at least mention it.

Lukkas clearly looked as if he didn't know what she was talking about. "Come again?"

"I talked to one of the crew members—a cameraman

named Eddie Harrington," she interjected. "From what I gathered, the whole crew thinks that you could walk on water if you really wanted to."

Lukkas frowned at her and shook his head. "Don't exaggerate, Hanna."

"I don't think I am," she told him. "If anything, I'm probably understating it. I don't know if you realize it, but you've got enough goodwill going for you here to mount a campaign for president of the United States if you wanted to."

For a second it looked as if he was just going to laugh in her face, Yohanna thought. And then he just shook his head, dismissing the very notion.

"Being a producer's rough enough, Hanna. Why in God's name would I want to put myself through something like that? And after the hell you go through, you wind up occupying the loneliest seat in the country. No thanks. I'm happy just making movies, giving people a reason to detach from their lives for a couple of hours and just let themselves be entertained."

"That cameraman I talked to also told me that you actually remember everyone's name."

"Is there a question in there somewhere?" he asked.

"Do you? Remember everyone's name," she clarified in case that had gotten lost in the shuffle.

Lukkas shrugged carelessly. "Seems like the right thing to do. Someone works for you, you should have the decency to know their name."

"No argument here," she told him. "But you are aware that that's pretty unique, aren't you?"

He shrugged again. "I really don't have the time to run any self-serving surveys," he told her. "I've got a movie to bring in on time and, if possible, underbudget."

"Well, I'm here to help with that in any way I can," she assured him a tad breathlessly.

Admittedly, she'd gotten a little caught up in the proceedings. Being around Lukkas seemed to do that. Not only that, but she found herself sneaking side glances at the man. Here, on the set, even when he wasn't issuing orders he seemed somehow larger than life.

Great, all you need is to fall for the guy. That'll end your career before it ever gets a chance to start, she chided herself. *Whatever you think you're feeling for this guy, you're not,* she silently emphasized, determined to get a firm grip on her overactive imagination.

"And you're sure about using Joanne Campbell?" Yohanna asked, getting back to the actress they'd discussed.

"Why?" he asked, curious as to why she would question something like this. "You don't think she's right for the part?"

"I have no idea about the part," Yohanna confessed. "I just want to be sure that you're sure."

He relaxed just the slightest touch. "Well, in that case, yes, I am."

"And what would you like to do about Monica Elliott?" She prodded.

That was simple as far as he was concerned. "Let her twist a little in the wind, then send her a text message telling her I've changed my mind and she can go do her other movie. Maybe she'll be nicer to the next director she works with on her next picture."

"You really think she can change her behavior?" Yohanna asked him skeptically.

"Hey, why not?" He was a firm believer in second chances. "I'm in the business of making fantasies, remember?"

"I remember." She brought up another topic that was, in her view, just as important. Possibly more so. "Have you eaten yet?"

Preoccupied, Lukkas was certain he'd heard his all-around assistant incorrectly.

"What?"

"Have you eaten?" she repeated. "I've noticed that you tend to get caught up in whatever you're doing and then you just forget to eat. Not recommended," she told him. "That catches up with you after a while—big-time."

"Auditioning for the part of my mother?"

Yohanna couldn't tell if he was amused or annoyed. She trod lightly.

"No. I just want to keep the job I have," she told him.

"Oh, didn't I tell you?" he asked, looking surprised at his own oversight.

Yohanna narrowed her eyebrows slightly as she looked at the producer, waiting for an explanation.

"Tell me what?" she prompted when he didn't immediately follow up on his previous question.

"That I've decided that you passed the test. You're hired on a permanent basis."

"No three-month probation?" she asked, wanting to be perfectly clear where she stood.

"Consider it month number four," Lukkas answered glibly.

He'd done it again. Left her stunned and falling behind, Yohanna thought. But this time, he also left her smiling to herself.

She figured she was making progress.

Chapter Seven

Hours later she was back on the plane, sitting next to Lukkas and waiting to make the sixty-minute trip to Bedford.

She'd just buckled up when she glanced out the window. The view, or lack thereof, suddenly sank in.

She could never live in a place like this.

"How do they stand it?" she asked Lukkas, staring out into the night.

Making one final notation in his notepad before tucking it back into his pocket, Lukkas slanted a look in her general direction, his attention split. "Stand what?" he asked.

"All that darkness." The fact that there was a new moon didn't help the scenario any. Yohanna suppressed a shiver that traveled along her spine. She'd never cared for the dark. As a child, she'd been afraid of it. "It's like being inside the bottom of midnight."

"Some people actually find the dark soothing," Lukkas told her.

"Not me," she responded with feeling. "The dark can hide things. I like being able to see what's out there at all times."

"At the moment, what's out there is darkness," he said wryly.

For a second she forgot that they were boss and assistant and just responded to him as if they were friends. Friends of long standing because she really was beginning to feel rather comfortable around Lukkas.

Blowing out a breath, she pretended that his teasing ruffled her feathers. "Very funny."

She saw the corners around his eyes crinkling as he made a guess about her childhood. "I bet you were afraid of the dark when you were a kid."

There was a time when she would have protested the observation despite the fact that it was right on the money. But that time was gone. She was more confident now in her own abilities, her own skills. She saw no reason to pretend that he had guessed wrong when he hadn't.

"My night-light was my best friend. It was in the shape of a Saint Bernard." A fond memory entered her mind. Her father had gotten it for her to help her get over her fear of the dark. "If it wasn't on, I couldn't sleep."

"Let me guess. You were a city kid."

She was and she was proud of it. "Born and bred," she affirmed.

Still, even city kids went to the country sometimes, he thought. He remembered his own childhood, squeezed in the backseat between two siblings and what felt like fourteen pointy elbows, desperately trying to look out the window to see where they were—and if they had gotten there yet.

"No long, grueling cross-country trips when your family went on vacation? No camping out or traveling through more desolate areas on your way to somewhere else?" he asked.

She shook her head. There had been no vacations in her childhood. "My father was a workaholic. The word *vacation* wasn't in his vocabulary. But he liked to take me to the local amusement park whenever he could," she told Lukkas in case he thought that she'd been deprived as a child. "We went on long bike rides, played ball in the field behind the high school. I didn't feel as if I was missing anything," she said, anticipating his possible next question. "It was a good childhood as far as it went."

The look on his face said he found that an odd way to put it. "And that was?"

"Until my dad died when I was twelve." An ironic smile slipped over her lips. "After that, my mother went to work and I helped out around the house to try to take up the slack. There was no time for vacations," she assured him.

Hers had been a no-nonsense kind of upbringing from that point on. Her mother had done her best, but there was no way she could have filled the void that her father had left behind.

Something in her voice had Lukkas asking, "You were close to your father?"

"I was," she admitted freely. Her father had understood her, had allowed her to be who she was. If he were still alive today, he wouldn't be trying to set her up with the sons and nephews of some of his friends the way her mother felt she had to. "He told me I could be anything

I wanted to be—as long as I was organized," she added with a laugh.

The sound of her laugh had Lukkas envisioning sunrises over fields of flowers. He smiled. "Is that how it all started? You being so very organized?" He embellished in case she didn't realize what he was referring to.

She nodded. "Yes, that's how it started. What little girl doesn't want to please her father?" Not that it took much. A clean bedroom; her homework done before dinner. These were all things that garnered her father's praise. She missed hearing it. "After he died…for a long time after that I secretly thought if I could just be organized enough, he'd come back." She laughed shortly, shaking her head. Had she *ever* really been that young and naive? "Drove my mother crazy. She'd put something down and before she could blink, I had it back in its place 'where it belonged.'"

She thought back to those days. "I guess to her I was bordering on OCD," she admitted, smiling to herself as she remembered a couple of incidents that had driven her mother particularly crazy. "Before you ask," she continued, "I got over it—partially because I knew what my little organizational campaign was doing to my mother. I knew that she missed my father, too. I didn't want to add to her sadness by making her think there was something wrong with me."

Yohanna understood that she had been monopolizing the conversation. And sharing much too much.

"Sorry," she apologized. "I have a habit of babbling." She felt herself flushing a bit. "You should have stopped me."

The extra color in her cheeks intrigued him. "Why? You gave me some insight into what makes you tick. I thought it was interesting."

And what makes you tick, Lukkas? Yohanna found herself wondering. *What can I ask you without making it look like I'm being overly nosy?*

"Besides," he continued with just a tiny bit of triumph in his voice, "it distracted you."

"Distracted me? From what?"

He gestured toward the window on her left. "We're airborne and you didn't have to squeeze your armrests until they all but fell off."

He was right. They were flying and she hadn't even been aware of the takeoff.

Yohanna looked through her window now. Staring, she could just barely make out dots of lights scattered about in no particular pattern—she assumed they were coming from homes built along the terrain—far below her.

His question about her fears of the dark had taken her back into the past and she'd gotten so wrapped up in revisiting memories of her father, she hadn't even noticed the change in cabin pressure or the powerful surging feeling of ascent.

Still, she felt she had to at least pretend that she had conquered her feeling about takeoffs and didn't need to white-knuckle them anymore.

"Or here's a thought," she suggested. "Maybe I've just conquered my fear of flying."

An amused smile played along his lips. "There is that. Looks as though we'll make a real world traveler out of you yet, Hanna," Lukkas predicted.

They landed in Bedford a little more than an hour later.

Feeling the downward shift, Lukkas opened his eyes.

That was when he realized that he must have fallen asleep sometime in the past fifteen minutes or so.

The long day he and Yohanna had put in had finally caught up to him.

Stifling a yawn, he stretched as best he could in the limited amount of space he had, and then rotated his neck a little. It felt stiff. Served him right for falling asleep sitting up.

Turning his head toward Yohanna, he was surprised to see that she had fallen asleep, as well. Apparently the long day had caught up to her, too.

He was about to gently shake her by the shoulder to wake her when something had him pausing for a second.

Pulling back his hand, he just looked at Hanna for a long moment. She'd been a ball of energy today, never questioning anything he told her to take care of, just finding a way to get it done and quickly.

He knew she'd come to him without any experience in the world where he had made his mark and yet she'd adapted so well and so quickly, it was hard to believe she hadn't been part of the film industry from the very beginning.

And there was something more.

Looking at her like this, her features soft and at rest rather than animated, he could see why his director had thought she was an actress. Aside from being exceptionally attractive, there was something about this young woman…an inherent sweetness that instantly transcended any awkward period that usually existed between strangers as they slowly got to know one another.

Hanna had something, a quality that effortlessly and instantly broke down barriers. That same quality made her someone he instinctively knew he could not only count on but that she could be a confidante, a friend who wouldn't let him down. Someone who would keep his secrets and be there to lend him silent—and not so silent—support when that was what was called for.

Whoa, Lukkas-boy, you're tired and getting carried away here. She's here to take Janice's place, not Natalie's, he reminded himself, afraid of where this was all taking him.

Shutting down any further reaction—*unwanted* reaction, he underscored—buzzing around inside him, he put his hand on Hanna's shoulder and shook it ever so slightly.

When she went on sleeping, he did it a second time, a little more forcefully this time around.

"Time to get up, Hanna—unless you want to spend the night on the plane," he told her.

The sound of Lukkas's voice wove its way into the dream she was having and, along with the jarring motion she felt on her shoulder, abruptly made her come around.

Blinking, Yohanna opened her eyes. She was disoriented for a moment.

"You fell asleep."

It wasn't an accusation but a statement of fact. Nevertheless, it still made her feel like an idiot who had dropped the ball. On the job a little more than two weeks and she was already falling asleep around the boss.

Not exactly a good thing to have happen when it came time to review her job performance.

"I'm sorry. I guess I was more tired than I thought. Are we still in the air?" she asked. Blinking again to clear her vision, she tried to focus as she looked out the window. An array of lights, both near and far, greeted her.

We're home, Toto, she thought with just a touch of whimsy.

"I guess not," she said out loud, answering her own question. And then another thought struck her. "I didn't hold you up, did I?"

"We just landed," he told her. "You slept through that like a baby. See? I told you that you'd get used to it."

She was never one who accepted any form of flattery as if she deserved it. "We'll see how I do when I'm awake," Yohanna replied.

She started to get up and found that she couldn't.

"Um, you might want to unbuckle your seat belt," Lukkas suggested, pointing toward the belt that was still quite buckled in place. "I don't think you're quite strong enough to take the plane with you."

Chagrined, she pressed the release button on the belt—and found that although the buckle made the appropriate noises, it wouldn't separate itself from the metal tongue that had fit so easily into the slot an hour ago.

She tried pressing it again and was on the receiving end of the same result.

Lukkas was already on his feet. When he heard her murmuring in frustration under her breath, he turned around to see what was wrong. He was surprised to find that she was still seated.

"Problem?" he asked.

"I think the seat belt doesn't want me to leave," she quipped drily.

"Let me have a look at it." Sitting next to her again, Lukkas tried to depress the lock and found that it just wouldn't budge. "Let's try this again," he said, seeming to address the words to the inanimate object rather than to her.

His hands on the seat belt, he applied more pressure as he tried to work the ends apart.

That had him accidentally brushing against places that he wouldn't have normally been in contact with—but he had no choice.

Yohanna shifted a little, not because she felt cramped, but because, as Lukkas was trying to free her from the uncooperative seat belt, he seemed to be unaware of the fact that his hands were brushing against her thighs, which in turn caused a heated chain reaction within her.

She was doing her very best not to notice.

She was failing.

Yohanna bit the inside of her cheek, struggling to think of other things.

Struggling to regulate the way she was breathing, as well.

Maybe if she didn't like the man as much as she did, if she actually *dis*liked him, she could easily block the warm shock waves he was unsuspectingly causing to dance all over her body.

But she *did* like him and consequently she *did* feel something spreading through her. Something she knew she shouldn't be feeling—definitely something she *couldn't* react to.

She vehemently didn't want to be one of *those* women; women who slept with their bosses as casually as they changed their clothes.

For his part, Lukkas was trying his very best not to notice that, try as he might not to, he kept brushing his hand against her, fleetingly touching her in places reserved for a lover's caress.

Tendering an apology might be too embarrassing for her, so he pretended not to be aware of it.

But he was.

Exceedingly so.

He could feel the charged electricity crackling between them all the way from the roots of his hair up to the very tips.

This reaction was purely physical and only happening because he hadn't been with a woman since his wife's death. He had never been one of those people who felt some unbridled need to sow wild oats fast and furiously anywhere and anytime he had the opportunity.

To him, relationships were tantamount to the experience, and he hadn't had a relationship since Natalie had died in that senseless crash.

Sitting back, he shook his head. "It's really stuck." He rolled the problem over in his head. "I guess I'm going to have to take drastic measures," he told her.

And just what did he mean by "drastic"?

"You're not leaving me here, are you?" she asked, looking at him uncertainly.

"As a sacrifice to the airplane gods?" he asked with a genuine laugh. "No, what I meant by that is that I'm going to have to cut the belt. Wait here," he told her, getting up again.

"It's not as if I have a choice," she called after him, frustrated and annoyed that she couldn't free herself without all this extra added effort.

She heard Lukkas laugh in response.

He came back ten minutes later, a pair of heavy-duty shears in his hand.

"I was getting worried," she confessed. "You were gone longer than I thought you'd be."

"You'd be surprised how hard it is to find a pair of scissors on a single-engine plane," he told her.

He sat to be closer to her when he made the necessary surgical cut. "Okay, now hold still," he instructed just before he got started.

"The idea of dancing around the cabin has a certain drawback at the moment," she told him, watching as he slipped one of the blades underneath the contrary seat belt.

She held her breath as she saw him grip the scissor handles and very slowly cut through the belt.

The latter was thicker than she had thought and the process was a slow one because, she assumed, he was trying not to cut her, as well.

In what felt like an eternity later, the two sides of the seat belt finally separated, freeing her from her gripping prison.

"You're free," he declared. "This makes you my very first official damsel in distress that I've rescued." He frowned as he looked at the severed belt. "Sorry you had to go through that."

"As long as you got me free, that's all that matters," Yohanna told him, very relieved that it was all over with and that she could finally get off the plane. "Thank you!"

Impulsively, going with the moment, Yohanna stood up on her toes and brushed her lips against his cheek.

Or at least that was her intent when she started.

Chapter Eight

Caught off guard by her closeness and the feel of something whisper soft and silky against his cheek, Lukkas automatically turned his head toward the source of that softness.

And just like that, it wasn't his cheek that her lips were touching. It was his *lips*.

A sense of propriety urged him to pull back. To mumble some sort of an apology even though he hadn't been the one to initiate the action that lay behind this situation.

But needs that far outweighed that sense of right and wrong prohibited him from stepping away from something he'd been missing these past few years. For the first time in all those months, the loneliness that haunted everything he did, that haunted all his waking hours, actually disappeared. The darkness that had hovered over his spirit moved aside and suddenly, just for a second, as he made this intimate contact with another human being, the sun flooded into every aching corner of his soul.

She tasted of strawberry and sweetness.

Most of all, she tasted of hope and, just possibly, salvation.

His salvation.

Horrified at what Lukkas probably thought she was trying to do, Yohanna ordered herself to pull back. All she had wanted to do was to thank him. Granted, this extra step had been an impulsive one on her part, but she hadn't meant for it to turn into anything else, especially not this.

Oh, but it had.

Big-time.

Instead of expressing simple gratitude, she found herself experiencing a wild surge within her veins that she had, until just this very moment, thought was merely the product of overimaginative writers who clearly dabbled in fiction, creating mythical scenarios that could not possibly be achieved in real life.

Except that they could.

Because she was having just such a reaction right now.

She still knew her own name, but as for anything else—where she was, what time it was, things like that— it was all hazy and even now was swiftly dissolving in the heat her body insisted on generating.

Yohanna had no idea how long the kiss continued. One eternity, maybe two. What she did know was that she had never felt this alive before. She felt like someone who could leap over tall buildings, who could do wonderful, wondrous things.

Without being fully aware of what she was actually

doing, she slipped her arms around Lukkas's neck. At that moment she felt his arms tightening around her, felt him bringing her closer so that her body swayed into his. That, in turn, ignited every single inch of her.

She wanted the moment, the kiss, to go on forever. She had never felt this alive before.

And then, as unintentionally as it began, it was over.

One of them had stepped back.

Had it been her?

Or maybe him?

She wasn't sure. One minute, they were all but bound to one another, utterly connected at the lips.

The next, they weren't.

"A simple handshake would have sufficed," Lukkas heard himself saying.

He'd seen the uncertain look in her eyes and knew he had to set the tone if they were ever going to move past this. If he was being honest with himself, all he really wanted to do was to kiss her again, to take her home and get to know every single inch of her.

Slowly.

But that wasn't possible or advisable on so many levels.

"What?"

Stunned, Yohanna looked at him. She replayed his words in her head. "Oh." Belatedly, she realized that he was teasing her and giving her a way to save face at the same time.

She silently blessed him for it.

"Okay, the next time I find myself trapped in my seat and you come to my rescue, I'll remember to shake your hand. How's that?" she asked him, playing along.

Lukkas nodded as he escorted her from the plane and down the metal stairs. Her heels hitting the metal made a rhythmic staccato sound.

"It's been a *long* day. Let's get you home." When he saw her slanting a startled look at him, he clarified, "*Your* home."

"Oh." She was relieved—and yet somehow, just on the fringes of her mind was another feeling lurking.

Disappointment.

Determined not to have Lukkas harbor any sort of doubts about the way she saw her actual job description and the subsequent performance evaluation that would eventually come, Yohanna threw herself into her work, determined to be the ultimate employee. It wasn't hard. She was good at this.

She came in early, stayed late and, bit by bit, brought complete order to what had otherwise threatened to dissolve into an utterly chaotic mess where nothing of any importance could be located—easily or otherwise— when it was needed.

She took to the work waiting to be done around her with amazing precision, organizing Lukkas's schedules, his meetings, all the while making certain that there were no overlaps and that none of the people Lukkas dealt with fell through the cracks.

And as always, she kept lists.

Lists of the people he could count on for financial backing for his project no matter what, and lists of people who needed to be wooed a little.

Or a lot.

In addition, she began to compile files on each of these people, noting their likes, their dislikes, their affiliations as well as the names and ages of their family members. In short, she did whatever it took to round out the mental picture for Lukkas so that he knew exactly who he was dealing with and just how to deal with them. Her research allowed him to always remain two steps ahead of anyone he interacted with.

The first time she showed him what she had worked up—and it was always going to be a work in progress, she assured him, since new people came into his life all the time—Lukkas found himself all but speechless.

The amount of time and effort she had to have put into organizing his life was astonishing.

"You did all this?" he marveled as Yohanna scrolled through the information on one of his new associates, a man who had come on board for the film Lukkas had produced just last spring.

Yohanna curbed the desire to tell him that the tooth fairy was behind all this. She wasn't sure if he could take a joke—or reject it because it wasn't of his own making.

"Yes," she replied instead.

She could see by his expression that he found the work she'd done to be extensive. In her opinion, it had to be. Otherwise, why else bother putting it together in the first place?

"Is Eli the only one you've worked up like this?"

Instead of answering him, Yohanna went back a couple of screens on the laptop, stopping when she pulled up the directory that she had created.

Silently, she scrolled down all the entries.

For the moment it seemed as if there were too many to count.

"When did you have time for all this?" Lukkas asked.

She shrugged. "I found pockets of time here and

there." And then she elaborated a little for him. "I did it when I wasn't inputting your storyboard."

"You did *what* to my storyboard?" he asked uncertainly, glancing at the item under discussion. The storyboard was off to the extreme left-hand side so it would be out of everyone's way until needed.

A film's storyboard was literally a large board on which drawings of the movie were pinned in their proper sequential order. It was the entire movie summed up as succinctly as possible. The director used it to help remind himself of the movie's ultimate focus or message.

Lukkas had asked her just to put up the drawings in their proper sequence.

She was obviously not referring to the corkboard that could be wheeled onto the set if he needed to have it brought there.

"I made up a virtual storyboard and saved it onto a USB drive as well as your smartphone. That way, you can always access it and make changes no matter where you are."

"You sure you never worked in the industry before?" Lukkas asked, scrutinizing her. She had such natural instincts about what was necessary—and what wasn't—he was having a hard time believing that she'd been a complete novice just a few weeks ago.

"I'm sure. I just know how to anticipate a boss," Yohanna replied, flashing her take-no-prisoners smile at him.

"Oh, really?" His tone had her bracing herself, instinctively knowing that he had just decided to throw her a curve. Thinking of it as a challenge, she was ready for anything. "Did your powers of anticipation allow you to anticipate being asked to that premiere and the party afterward that I have to attend?"

Yohanna was well aware of the premiere and subsequent party Lukkas had to attend since he'd had her call each of the major stars in the movie to coax, cajole or plead with them, doing whatever she had to do to get them to promise to appear at the showing.

She had just assumed he'd already had someone to go with. This was a whole new twist she hadn't prepared for and, for a moment, she was at a complete loss as to how to respond.

"You're asking me to attend?" Yohanna asked in disbelief.

He gave her a look that whispered of moderately bridled impatience. "I'm pretty sure I was just speaking English, so yes, I'm asking you to attend the premiere— and the party—with me."

"Why?" The question had slipped out like a stunned whisper.

This man was one of Hollywood's most eligible bachelors. What was the man doing, asking her to attend a premiere with him? *And* the party afterward? He could easily have his pick of any one of a large number of stunning women. She couldn't begin to compete with any of those.

So why was he asking *her* to come with him to this premiere?

"Because if I go alone, aside from speculation about my playing the lonely widower, since I'm the producer and I'm under seventy with all my own teeth, I will be a walking target for any starlet on the rise and willing to go to great lengths to get to the top of the heap. I'll also be easy prey for any backer who has a female relative he'd like to see married or at least involved with someone."

"And you don't want to be that someone," Yohanna ventured.

Lukkas nodded. "Give that young lady a prize," he declared like a carnival barker.

"So you want me to be your beard," she summarized astutely.

The label conjured up the wrong image—at least in his head. "I'd rather think of you as my entanglement repellent."

Yohanna laughed at his choice of words. "That makes me sound like a bug spray."

Lukkas shrugged. He went to his desk to take something out of one of the lower drawers. "Call it any way you see it as long as you're ready to be picked up at five-thirty tomorrow."

She felt her stomach quickening. She wasn't quite as blasé about things as she would have liked to portray. "I know this sounds clichéd, but I don't have a thing to wear for something of this magnitude."

If she thought that would be the end of it, she was sadly mistaken. Lukkas was not a man who gave up easily and he could be just as stubborn as she could.

Possibly more so.

Lukkas reached into his back pocket, took out his wallet and almost without looking selected a credit card, which he then in turn handed to her.

"Here," he told her. "Get something that'll make a good showing at tomorrow's premiere of *Diamonds and Dust*—but not so much that it takes the focus off the movie," he warned.

Yohanna stared at the credit card. Specifically, she

stared at his name embossed on the credit card. She had her own credit cards, but since she had taken over issuing payment checks for his bills, she knew that her cards had a far lower cut-off ceiling than his did.

She looked back up at him incredulously. "You're kidding, right?"

"If I were kidding, laughter would be involved somewhere. Real laughter, not nervous laughter," he attested. "You hear any?"

Yohanna slowly moved her head from side to side. "No."

"Then, I'm not kidding," he concluded. He glanced at the card he had just given her. The same one she was still clutching as if she expected it to either burst into flame or levitate away from her. "You want to take a few hours off to go shopping?"

Her first response was to say yes, but then her stubborn streak kicked in. She was not about to take advantage of either him or the situation—no matter how tempting it might be.

"No, I'll take care of it on my own time," she answered.

Admittedly, Yohanna was still a little shell-shocked over what had just happened, but she instinctively knew what to do to take care of herself—even around dropdead gorgeous men, a club that Lukkas clearly belonged to.

"Have it your way—you do know that there's such a thing as being *too* good to be true, right?" Lukkas asked her.

Lukkas started to leave his office when he stopped to impart one last thought on the subject. "Oh, and by the way, do something with your hair."

Her hand automatically came up to touch the back of her hair. Did he find it lacking? Distracting? Or— what? She needed to know to understand how to remedy the situation.

"My hair?"

"Yes. Wear it up," he answered, waving one hand around in the air as if he were a wand-wielding fairy godmother, able to make things do his bidding with a flick of his wrist. "This is going to be on the formal side."

"Are you *sure* you want me to go with you?" she asked, hoping that he'd change his mind at the final moment.

Lukkas rephrased her question and turned it into an answer. "Am I sure I don't want to be inundated with women who, for one reason or another, see me as a means to an end? Yes, I'm sure. Think of it as part of your job description," he instructed.

"*What* part?" she challenged.

"The part that comes under 'miscellaneous,'" he answered as he left the office.

She stared at his credit card for several moments before she finally put it away into her own wallet. Her fingertips felt almost icy as she handled the card. It represented a great deal of power in its own right, she thought, tucking the wallet with Lukkas's card into the depths of her purse, otherwise known—according to Lukkas—as "no man's land."

A quick but intense review of the contents of her closet that night only told Yohanna what she already knew—she did *not* own a single suitable dress she could wear to a premiere, certainly not something that wouldn't stand out like a sore thumb when she crossed the red carpet beside Lukkas.

She shook her head as she closed her closet. This all still felt so surreal to her. Her, at a premiere. With one of Hollywood's most eligible bachelors. Who would've thunk it?

Whenever she found herself in unfamiliar waters and treading madly, her natural inclination had always been to seek help. But in this case, the only one she could actually turn to would be her mother.

However, she knew if she did, while she would be playing into her mother's fantasy, she would also be opening up such a huge can of worms, she wouldn't have a prayer in hell of ever being able to close it again.

Besides, her mother had already called her several times since she'd started working for Lukkas. The calls all revolved around the same issue. Her mother wanted progress reports and, more specifically, her mother wanted to know exactly how far she had progressed in her relationship with Lukkas.

That there *was* no relationship in progress other than their professional one was not something she seemed to be able to get across to her mother.

It was clear that the woman was absolutely *starving* for romance. Romance in *her* life, not actually in her own, Yohanna thought ruefully. Her mother was one of those women who lived vicariously through their offspring.

Not for the first time, Yohanna wished that she had a sister, or at the very least a cousin she could hide behind or possibly divert her mother's attention to.

But, knowing her mother, she supposed that would blow up in her face, as well.

She could just hear her mother saying, "Why can't you get married and have a husband and kids like your cousin Rachel?"

No, she was better off this way, with no one to be compared to, Yohanna decided.

But she still needed help.

Mentally, she reviewed the women she could call for some sort of advice in a situation like this. And then she realized that there was only one logical candidate.

She fervently hoped that she wouldn't be disturbing the woman, but really, if it hadn't been for her, most likely she would still be sitting in her condo—a condo that would look far less tidy than it did now—out of work and out of hope.

Her present dilemma was both Cecilia's fault and her gift to her, Yohanna thought. In any case, she felt she could attain a sympathetic ear from the woman—as well as a minimum of questions. Cecilia was obviously the kind of lady who cared, but by the same token, she wasn't the kind to pry or to insert herself into someone's life— possibly not even when invited to do so.

Making up her mind, Yohanna picked up the phone and called Cecilia.

Chapter Nine

"Not that I'm not honored as well as touched that you called me to help you pick out something special to wear to the premiere of Mr. Spader's new movie, but why isn't your mother here instead of me, dear?"

After attempting to repress the question during the drive to Rodeo Drive and an exclusive boutique she was familiar with, Cecilia's curiosity had gotten the better of her. She knew that if she found out her daughter had gone to another older woman for advice rather than come to her, she would have been heartbroken.

Cecilia had tried to sound as casual as she could, broaching the question as they walked into the boutique.

Yohanna loved her mother dearly but, in her estimation, that didn't mean she had to put up with her mother's theatrics, and there *would be* theatrics if the woman found out about this.

"Because," Yohanna patiently explained, "if my mother finds out that I'm going to be attending something with my boss that involves walking across a red carpet, I guarantee that five minutes later, she's going to be hiring someone to write the words *Mr. Spader, please marry my daughter, Yohanna* across the sky."

Two sleek, tastefully made up saleswomen started walking in their direction. Cecilia waved them back. To Yohanna's astonishment, the women retreated.

Cecilia obviously had clout here.

"Now, dear," Cecilia was saying, commenting on the scenario Yohanna had just painted for her. "You're exaggerating—"

Yohanna laughed drily as she went to the first display of evening gowns. "No, I'm not. You obviously haven't met my mother."

"No, I have not," Cecilia admitted. "But even if I haven't—"

Yohanna proceeded as if Cecilia hadn't attempted to continue. "She's the one who told me that a real woman cleans her own house and said I was throwing money away on a cleaning service."

Cecilia winced just a tiny bit. "Ah, an old-fashioned woman."

"If the fashions are from the 1900s, then, yes, she is an old-fashioned woman. She is also a very determined woman. Right now, what she's determined about is to marry me off to someone. Anyone short of Attila the Hun is a viable possible candidate. In my mother's eyes I'm in a very precarious place, teetering on the edge of a downhill slope that'll send me sliding right into becoming an old maid."

Cecilia smiled indulgently at her. "Nobody really uses that term anymore, dear."

But Yohanna could only smile, as if her point had been made. "Like I said, you haven't met my mother. What do you think of this one?" she asked, holding one of the gowns up against herself.

"It's not your color," Cecilia pronounced, dismissing the gown with a wave of her hand. Yohanna returned it to its original space as Cecilia began to look through the various gowns. "Have you stopped to think that this event might be covered by one of those cable channels and the camera might pick up your presence there? Since you're attending the premiere with the movie's producer, I can guarantee that cameras will be trained on you.

"This does assume, of course, that your mother watches these kinds of programs. If she doesn't, then you're home free." Cecilia looked at her face and drew her own conclusion. "She watches these shows, doesn't she?"

Yohanna could only nod, feeling a definite pressure from the weight accumulating on her chest. "But every now and then, she does miss one occasionally." There was a breathless, hopeful note in her voice as she mentally crossed her fingers.

"Then, for your sake, I hope she's busy watching something else," Cecilia replied. She debated over a gown, then shrugged and moved it aside. "It's Saturday night. Does she go out with your father, or perhaps some friends?" Cecilia asked hopefully as she went on looking and rejecting gowns one after the other.

Yohanna could only look on, leaving the selection entirely in the older woman's hands because she felt she needed someone steadier than she was to make the final decision.

"My dad died years ago," she said, replying to Cecilia's question. "But Mom does go out with a couple of her girlfriends sometimes. I don't know if it's on Saturday nights or not."

"All you can do is play the odds, dear— That one," Cecilia suddenly exclaimed, gravitating toward a long, light blue gown covered with sequins of a single silver color. The sequins winked and blinked, casting their own beams of light.

Removing it from its hanger, Cecilia offered the gown to Yohanna. "This is perfect for you," she pronounced without any fanfare, cocking her head as if she was studying Yohanna for the first time. "The blue brings out your eyes and it makes you come alive—I mean, more than you already are," Cecilia amended tactfully.

"Understood," Yohanna replied, not wanting the woman to worry about hurting her feelings.

Her mother certainly never had such concerns. There were times that she was convinced her mother went directly for the jugular just to keep her in line.

Too bad it hadn't worked. She was still her own person. She hadn't been brainwashed into believing her mother's ancient mantra. That a woman wasn't complete until she was married.

She was complete, Yohanna thought fiercely. Moreover, she was doing just fine without a male in her life.

And maybe just a little more fine than that, she silently insisted.

"Try it on, dear," Cecilia coaxed, still holding out the gown to her.

Beaming, Yohanna took the gown from Cecilia and headed to the first changing room.

It took her all of three minutes to get out of her own clothes and into the gown Cecilia seemed to have inadvertently stumbled across.

And then it took her an extra two minutes to tear herself away from the reflection in the mirror that she found awe-inspiring and overwhelming.

"Are you all right in there, dear?" Cecilia inquired, raising her voice. Yohanna was taking a long time inside the changing room.

"Just fine," Yohanna called back.

She was still mesmerized by what she saw—a reflection that just couldn't have possibly been her. Instead, the reflection was of a startlingly sexy woman who just happened to be looking back at her.

Yohanna could hardly tear her eyes away, afraid if she did, when she looked back, the reflection would be gone and she'd be left in its stead.

Plain, reliable Yohanna.

She turned slowly to the side, exposing the floor-to-upper-thigh slit in the gown. She absolutely *loved* this gown.

Holding her breath, she ventured out of the change room to present herself to the woman who had brought her here in the first place. She wanted to hear Cecilia's opinion even as she crossed her fingers, hoping that Cecilia would give her stamp of approval on this one. Granted, she could buy it if she had no choice, but in this virgin effort to get just the right gown, she knew she needed backup.

Someone to tell her she was right.

Besides, it would be rather rude not to ask Cecilia

what she thought of the gown. After all, she had been the one who had found the gown.

As for herself, she was half in love with the gown and on her way to proposing to it.

"So?" Yohanna asked hopefully as she very slowly turned in a full circle for the woman's benefit. "What do you think?"

Cecilia's pleased smile said it all. "I think Mr. Spader is going to need a cold shower *before* and *after* the premiere. Also after the party that'll follow."

She'd almost forgotten about that. Maybe Lukkas wouldn't want to attend. "Are you sure there's a party after the premiere?" she asked Cecilia.

"Honey, there is *always* an after-party," Cecilia answered knowingly. "A party before. A party after. The people in the film industry work hard at what they do, so when it's all said and done, they like to party hard, too, sort of to balance everything out," Cecilia explained. "And also because there's always that chance that after the party's over, nothing further comes their way. This is a very, very hard business people have consigned themselves to."

Cecilia paused to take a breath and then smiled warmly again, her eyes crinkling. "I think I forgot to mention the most important part—you look perfect."

Yohanna could feel her cheeks growing warmer. Compliments always embarrassed her. "Thank you— even though that's not possible."

"Why not?" Bemused, Cecilia challenged her opinion, but amicably so.

She'd felt like an ugly duckling most of her life. Her mother had branded her as such, lamenting that it would be difficult to find her a husband because of that. To have

Cecilia compliment her this way was flattering—but it almost didn't feel real.

"Because nothing human is perfect, no matter how hard we might try."

"All right, I'll amend my statement," Cecilia said indulgently. "You're as close to perfect as possible." Cocking her head just a shade, the woman looked at her. "Happy?"

Maybe that reflection in the mirror really *was* her.

"Deliriously," Yohanna responded.

"Wear that," Cecilia instructed, indicating the gown. "And you'll knock 'em all dead," she promised.

Happy that she'd found something and relieved that she didn't have to go on searching for the "right" thing to wear for the better part of the day, Yohanna started to go back to the change room. As she walked, she glanced at the price tag attached to the garment and stopped dead in her tracks.

Surprised, Cecilia came closer to her. "Is something wrong?"

She was still staring at the price tag, all but shell-shocked. "This dress costs around the same amount of money it would take to feed a third world nation for a week."

There was an extremely practical side to Cecilia. "You're not paying for it, are you?" she asked, softness creeping into her voice despite the harsh nature of the question she'd just asked.

"Mr. Spader gave me his credit card," Yohanna confessed.

"Then, charge away," Cecilia urged with a laugh as she nudged her into the change room. "In your producer's pretty green eyes, the money is being put to good use."

As she changed, Yohanna still thought it incredibly wasteful to be using that much money to purchase a simple gown.

"But this money could feed so many kids," she protested, exiting the change area.

"And it will, eventually," Cecilia assured her. "Spader is a very compassionate man. If someone calls him with a hard-luck story, Lukkas Spader is on the phone, calling one or more of his security team to find the caller, and then he delivers the money to them in person."

Cecilia was only repeating what Theresa had already told her about the man. Her friend had been impressed with the size of the producer's heart in an industry that notoriously had no heart.

"Now buy that gown and give that man something beautiful to look at," Cecilia instructed.

Yohanna smiled as she went up to the register.

Directed by Cecilia's keen instincts, Yohanna found herself going to several other stores, notably Neiman Marcus, to buy accessories that she hadn't realized she needed for the night ahead. New shoes. A tiny purse hardly big enough to house a lipstick and a house key. A wrap to throw on her shoulders in case the evening grew chilly. All these things, Cecilia had maintained, were necessary to complete the portrait of a woman who could easily fit into Lukkas's world.

After a while Yohanna had the feeling she was on an endless treadmill and that the shopping would never end.

And then finally, finally—after nearly giving up hope—she was home.

Home with only a few hours to get ready. Her nerves all but went into overdrive. Already worried that she'd somehow wind up putting her worst foot forward, Yohanna tried not to dwell on anything negative.

The butterflies in her stomach were already threatening to hollow out her insides with their ever-increasing wingspan as they perpetually took off and landed.

Being Yohanna, she was ready long before she needed to be. That left her time to pace and to anticipate the worst. The more she did either, the more nervous she became even though she really hadn't thought that was actually possible.

Willing Lukkas to come early, she kept looking at her watch to see how much time had passed.

The hands on her watch were moving so slowly, she felt certain that the minute hand had been dipped in honey.

The inside of her mouth was dry again—something that had been going on all day—actually, ever since he'd asked her to accompany him.

The moment she turned away from the window and began to head to the kitchen, the doorbell rang. She nearly jumped out of her skin, grateful that no one had been there to take in the sight.

Taking a breath, she went to answer the door.

Fully prepared to see Lukkas when she opened the door, she offered him a cheerful "Hi."

"Wow," he heard himself say in response. When the door had opened to admit him, he'd fully expected to see the young woman he'd hired three weeks ago, and instead he was all but bowled over by the absolutely gorgeous woman standing in the doorway.

"Hanna?" Lukkas asked hesitantly.

He couldn't be certain it was her.

The woman standing right in front of him looked like Hanna and yet didn't.

"It's me," she assured him, opening the door wider for him to enter.

Pleasure spiraled through her as she noted the way Lukkas was looking at her.

"I take it by your initial comment that you like the gown."

"Like it?" he echoed. "I think I'm in love with it. You look nothing short of fantastic," he told her with genuine feeling in his voice.

She decided she might as well tell him now rather than later. After all, he was the one putting up money to fund the next project. She couldn't just take more from him because she thought the gown was gorgeous.

"It was awfully expensive," she apologized. "I saved all the tags and, if I'm super careful, I can reattach them and take everything back to the store so that you can get your money refunded."

He caught himself wondering if she was for real and then decided she was. That in turn made her a rarity. And special in his eyes.

"Number one, I don't want my money back," he told her. "If you don't want to keep this gown after the premiere, I guess we can return it. Any money we get will be forwarded to the charity of your choosing. Although, personally, I vote to make it simple and just keep the gown. You never know when you might need to show up somewhere wearing something drop-dead gorgeous to win over the crowd.

"Number two. The sight of you in that dress is well worth any investment into this evening that I've had to make. Now loosen up a little, smile and have fun. You're walking into a movie theater, not walking your last mile to get a lethal injection," he reminded her, then prodded a little further. "Why don't you try smiling? In case you didn't know—" and he was certain that being Hanna, she didn't "—you've got a really terrific smile."

Without thinking she raised her hand and brushed her fingertips along her lips, as if that could somehow allow her to "see" herself the way he saw her.

"I do?" she asked a little hesitantly. "My mother always said I put too much teeth into my smile. I guess it made me a little self-conscious." *Or a lot*, she added silently.

"They're your teeth," he told her kindly, and then reminded her, "You can put them anywhere you want to."

She laughed. "You make it sound as if they were false teeth I could just take out and leave lying around somewhere."

"I was hoping to coax a smile out of you with that."

"You don't have to coax," she told him warmly. "The only thing I want from you is to give me your word that you won't leave me stranded at this premiere."

His eyebrows drew together. "Why would I?" he asked, perplexed. "The whole purpose of taking you is so that you can run interference for me, be my shield against a possible wall of female humanity. If I wanted to wander off and leave you stranded, I wouldn't have asked you to come with me to begin with." Lukkas lowered his head a little so that he could gaze directly into her eyes. "Okay?"

"Okay," she echoed, sounding a little more heartened than she had a few minutes ago.

"Then, Cinderella, your coach awaits," he told her, putting out his elbow so that she could hook her arm through it.

* * *

They arrived at the movie theater—originally *the* Grauman's Chinese Theatre, Yohanna noted with a secret thrill—by stretch limousine. She found the ride exceedingly smooth, but then she was so focused on the evening ahead that she felt she wouldn't have noticed if there'd been a raccoon in the limo with them—unless he'd gotten out of line.

The driver was the first to exit the black, highly polished vehicle. He hurried around to the back and opened the door for her and for Lukkas.

Yohanna got out first.

The cries, calls from fans and photographers vying for their attention, formed almost a deafening wall of noise. She found it almost dizzying in its intensity.

"Don't worry," Lukkas told her, whispering the words into her ear so that she was able to hear them. "You'll get used to it after a while."

She didn't see how.

It was all very different on this side of the TV monitor. Whenever she caught a glimpse of a premiere on TV, it seemed moderately exciting and a tad boring.

This…this was just completely overwhelming. *Boring* was the last adjective she would have applied to the event.

When she suddenly felt Lukkas threading his arm through hers to lead her down the red carpet—*the* red carpet—instant relief flooded through her.

He was still with her.

Just as he'd promised.

Chapter Ten

It was, Yohanna thought the next moment, not unlike being in the center of an all but blinding light show.

Along with the raised voices of reporters who were all vying to snare the majority of Lukkas's attention, she heard the lower somewhat rhythmic sound of cameras going off, automatically snapping photographs while other cameras were videotaping their every move until the next stellar subject came into view.

Her natural inclination was to pick up speed and get away from the noise, the reporters and the flashing lights of their cameras as quickly as possible.

But she wasn't here as herself; she was here in connection with Lukkas. This was his night, not hers, and she was well aware that whatever she did, good or bad, would ultimately reflect on him. That was just the way things were.

So despite the fact that she found being photographed almost nonstop from every single possible angle more than a little unsettling, she reminded herself that this wasn't about her. It was about Lukkas. She wasn't Yohanna Andrzejewski; she was the production assistant who Lukkas Spader had brought with him to this important Hollywood premiere. As such, she had to convey the proper message as well as conduct herself accordingly. In no way was she to act as if she was his "date" beyond the fact that she was attending this premiere with him.

A second later she realized that not only cameras but questions were being directed at her.

"How long have you and Lukkas been dating?" a disembodied voice, a shade louder than the rest, asked.

Here we go, Yohanna thought. She took a breath as inconspicuously as possible, then answered, "We're not." Yohanna flashed a smile in the general direction the question had come from. "I work for Mr. Spader. Bringing me with him to this premiere is just his generous way of thanking me for doing what he considered to be an excellent job." She glanced toward Lukkas as she added, "I'm really excited to be here."

"How about it, Lukkas? Is what she just said true? Or are you really just trying to put one over on the public?" the same loud voice asked.

He had been the subject of endless speculation ever since his wife's funeral. After almost three years he was prepared for these kinds of questions.

"I wouldn't dream of insulting the viewing public that way. The only fantasies I create can be seen right up there on the screen," Lukkas replied genially.

There were more questions, fired at them from any one of a number of people swarming around them. Lukkas politely dealt with several of them, and then, just as politely, begged off.

"That's all for now, guys. The movie's about to start and I make it a point never to be late for my own productions," he explained amicably. His hand on the small of Yohanna's back, Lukkas gently ushered her along with him.

Moving briskly beside him, Yohanna didn't allow herself to breathe a sigh of relief until they were finally inside the theater.

Turning to Lukkas, she confessed, "I had no idea that reporters were this intense." Red carpet or not, going from the limousine to the inside of the theater was almost like being subjected to a baptism by fire.

"Actually, I think they were taking it easier than they normally do," he told her. "The reporters and paparazzi aren't used to me attending premieres with anyone. Not in the past few years anyway," he added, an unmistakable touch of sadness in his voice. He pushed it aside as he smiled at her, approval evident in his eyes. "By the way, you handled yourself very nicely."

He'd made the last sentence sound almost like an afterthought, but the fact that he'd said it at all made her feel as if she was successfully doing her job. She focused on that rather than the fact that his hand was still against the small of her back, ever so lightly guiding her through the lobby.

Warm, delicious pinpricks of heat were darting through her.

"Maybe I can add that to my résumé someday," she responded whimsically. "'Will shill on demand.'"

Laughing, Lukkas promised, "I'll give you a letter of recommendation when it comes time."

When it comes time.

Yohanna rolled the words over in her head, wondering if her actual days of being in the producer's employ were numbered.

The next moment she decided she wasn't going to think about that now. If that did turn out to be the case, it wouldn't be anything she hadn't already been through—and survived. For now, she intended to make herself totally indispensable to the man in every way possible, doing what she was good at.

What she needed to do right this minute was to not react to the feel of his arm around her shoulders as he escorted her inside the actual theater where the huge IMAX screen was located. Shivers were moving up and down her spine, making every inch of her acutely aware of the man beside her.

And she definitely wasn't thinking of him as her employer at the moment.

C'mon, Yohanna, focus. Focus.

The house lights were beginning to dim. She felt Lukkas's arm slip from her shoulders. One contact substituted for another. Before she knew it, he was taking her hand.

Her heartbeat quickened even though she silently insisted that Lukkas was merely trying to make sure she didn't stumble in the darkened theater.

"Our seats are up front," he whispered.

As if on cue, an usher appeared in front of them. He led the way, using a flashlight to illuminate the path down the aisle.

The theater was filled to capacity with not even standing room available, but as far as she was concerned, she and Lukkas were alone in the theater, making their way to the first row.

Progress was achieved in slow motion. The journey down the aisle to the first row felt like an eternity. The only theaters she had ever frequented vied with medium-size living rooms when it came to square footage. This theater was so large it could have swallowed up at least a dozen—if not more—of those theaters. Possibly also a few of the smaller towns.

And then, finally, they came to the row that matched the ticket stubs they'd been given, arriving just as the curtain was being drawn back. A giant dormant screen came into view.

"Just in time," Lukkas whispered, lowering his lips to her ear.

She was acutely aware of his breath as it lightly glided along her cheek and neck.

She struggled hard to keep a shiver from surfacing. She wasn't seventeen anymore, Yohanna silently insisted.

It didn't help.

"Just in time," she echoed, hoping that Lukkas couldn't hear the way her heart had started to pound. Threading her way into the row, Yohanna gratefully sank into her seat as the opening credits appeared on the screen.

Another shaky sigh of relief escaped her lips before she could stifle it. She crossed her fingers, hoping that Lukkas hadn't noticed.

"You never took your eyes off the screen the entire time," Lukkas commented as, nearly two and a half hours later, they made their way up the aisle to leave the theater.

Progress was slow going because it seemed as if every third person they passed wanted to congratulate the producer on the quality of the film he had shepherded into existence.

She told him what everyone else was saying. "It was a good movie."

Rather than gloat, he allowed his natural humility to take over. "You have to say that."

Moving ever closer to the double doors the ushers had opened, she spared him a glance. Didn't he know her at all? She would have thought with the man's keen perception, he would have had a bead on her character—good and bad—by now. Obviously not.

"The only thing I *have* to do is show up on time in the morning and put in a full day's work before I leave for the night," she pointed out. "Empty flattery was not in the job description. And how do you know I never took my eyes off the screen?" she asked. "Weren't *you* watching the movie?"

"I've seen it," he told her drily, then added honestly, "I was looking around to gauge everyone else's reaction to the movie." His voice didn't betray whether the answer to that had pleased him or had caused him concern.

The lights had gone up some, but for the most part, the theater was still rather dimly lit. He couldn't have been able to see far, she thought.

"Kind of dark for that, wasn't it?" she asked.

"Which was why I spent a lot of time looking at you," he told her simply.

That wasn't entirely true. Gauging Hanna's reaction to the movie was only part of the reason his attention had kept being drawn back to her. Something about the young woman kept tugging at him, a connection of sorts that he was both hesitant to explore and yet felt almost compelled to.

He was borrowing trouble, as his grandmother used to say, and his life was already too full. He didn't need any extra complications being wedged into it.

And yet…

And yet nothing, Lukkas reminded himself sternly. People were counting on him for their very livelihood. He had no time to stray off a path he had set down for himself three years ago. A path that was the only thing keeping him sane.

No sooner had he and Hanna finally reached the lobby than they were joined by a tall, blustery man who immediately took his hand and pumped it.

"Judging from the bits and pieces I've been picking up," Darren Thompson, the head of the studio that was set to distribute Lukkas's film throughout the country, told him, "it looks as though you've got yourself another winner on your hands, Spader."

"*We've* got another hopeful winner on our hands," Lukkas corrected. Aware of his abilities as well as the quality of what he produced, Lukkas was always cautiously optimistic in his statements. No one could fault a man for being cautious.

But they could tease him about it.

The studio executive shook his head. "For once in your life, Spader, cut loose, for heaven's sake." The man turned toward Yohanna with no warning. "Help me out here," Thompson requested. "Tell the man how good his movie is."

"I already did," Yohanna told the executive. "But Mr. Spader comes around at his own pace. Nothing anyone can do but wait until he catches up."

"I like her," Thompson said, nodding in Yohanna's direction as he clapped one wide, heavy paw of a hand on Lukkas's back. "Where did you find her and are there more like her?" he asked brightly. "I could use a few level heads working for me at the studio."

Yohanna answered for the producer, sparing him a possible awkward situation. "He found me under a rock labeled Organizer, and I'm one of a kind."

Amused, Thompson laughed heartily. "I believe that, I surely do. Careful, Spader, or I'll steal her away from you." He punctuated the so-called threat with a broad wink.

"Not anytime soon, you won't," Lukkas told him with a good-natured smile on his lips. "I still need her. She's got a lot of organizing left to do before I'm close to being a done deal."

Was he telling the truth or just running interference for her? she wondered. She knew which she hoped it was. But this was work, not pleasure, and she needed to remember that and act accordingly.

"We'll see," Thompson promised, his tone pregnant with self-confidence. "In the meantime, I'd keep her close if I were you."

Lukkas looked at her as they parted company with the studio executive. Close. Heaven knew the directive was appealing. He would have liked nothing better than to keep her close.

Which was exactly why he shouldn't.

This was the first woman he was reacting to since he'd lost Natalie. He had no doubt that this situation consti-tuted his version of a rebound. It would be insulting to his wife's memory and it would definitely be unfair to

Hanna if he allowed himself to begin what would only have an abrupt, unhappy ending in its future.

"Should I be worried?" he asked Yohanna, tongue in cheek.

Not certain if he was being serious or not, she decided her best bet was to act innocent until she could piece his question together.

"I don't know. Worried about what in particular?" she asked.

He put it as succinctly as possible. "That you'll jump ship."

He watched in fascination as the corners of her mouth curved, forming a smile that was all but irresistible in his opinion.

"Not while we're out in the middle of the ocean," she quipped. "Besides," she added on a serious note, "there's still too much to do and I never willingly leave a job half finished. So unless you're planning on letting me go any time soon, just let me do my job and everyone'll be happy."

They were in the theater lobby and discovered that even here the progress to the front doors was incredibly slow moving.

She knew he didn't like being forced to move at this pace. It couldn't even be described as crawling.

"Bet you're glad that this evening's over," she commented. How could so many glittering, beautiful people be crammed into such a small space? she wondered.

"You'd lose that bet on two counts," Lukkas informed her. "I'm not all that glad and the evening's not over."

She wasn't sure if she'd heard him correctly. "It's not?"

"No." He lowered his head to make sure that she heard

him. The noise level had gone up again. "We still have a party to attend, remember?"

She knew that there was an after-party, but she'd just assumed that he'd want to attend it without having her around. "I just thought—"

"Premieres are *always* followed by parties."

His tone of voice didn't leave any room for argument. She took her cue from that. Besides, Cecilia had said as much to her when they had gone shopping for her gown earlier. There was *always* a party.

"Right. What was I thinking?" she quipped, hoping that Lukkas wouldn't feel inclined to make a whimsical guess.

Lukkas allowed himself a short laugh. "The Shadow knows."

Obviously confused, Yohanna paused to look at him quizzically.

Lukkas realized the obscure reference had gone right over her head. "Sorry, that was way before your time—and mine, if you're wondering," he added quickly. "I was raised on old classic programs. *The Shadow* was an old, old radio program. The opening and closing lines were always—"

Yohanna nodded. They were finally outside the theater. After being inside for so long, the cool night air felt almost downright chilly. She pulled her wrap closer around her, silently blessing Cecilia's instincts.

"'Who knows what evil lurks in the hearts of men? The Shadow knows,'" she quoted.

The completely stunned expression on Lukkas's face pleased her.

"You're familiar with that?" Lukkas asked in disbelief.

"Guilty as charged." And then she admitted, "I'm a trivia buff."

Lukkas raised his hand, signaling their position to his limo driver. The same fans who had lined the streets earlier were still there, waiting to catch another glimpse of the film's celebrities.

"You are just full of surprises, Hanna," he told Yohanna with a wide, approving smile.

The limo pulled up, and rather than wait for the driver to hop out and open doors for them, Lukkas opened the rear door, gesturing for Yohanna to get in.

"C'mon, let's get this party over with," he urged. "With a little luck, I'll have you back, safe and sound, in your own bed by midnight, Cinderella."

"You're the boss," she said, sliding carefully into the limousine.

"For now," he agreed.

Yohanna wasn't sure just what he meant by that, but she thought it best to leave it alone. That way, she was able to put her own meaning to things without being disillusioned.

She had to admit she was pleasantly surprised that Lukkas remembered his initial promise to her even at the party. She'd expected him either to wander away or be drawn away by one of the myriad of people—men and most notably women—who were competing for his attention. But each time he did move on to talk to someone, Lukkas ushered her along with him.

And if, by some chance, someone was talking to her at the time, Lukkas waited until she was finished and the verbal exchange was over.

She caught herself thinking that it was almost as if they actually *were* a couple.

Almost.

But she knew there was a fine line between reality and make-believe—especially here, in the very birthplace of make-believe—and she knew the difference.

Still, it was hard not to fall into the very tempting trap of pretending, just for a little while, that things were the way they seemed rather than the way they actually were.

The party continued until after midnight.

Lukkas had checked with her a couple of times to see if she wanted—or was ready—to go home. But each time he asked, she convinced him that she was wide-awake and doing just fine.

Until she was fading and tired.

The next time he asked, she still made the proper protests, but this time he overrode her.

"Save your breath, Cinderella. I'm taking you home," he told her.

She didn't want to be the reason why he had to leave the party. As the producer of what was, by all indications, a blockbuster of a movie, this was his time to shine and she didn't want to spoil that for him. After all, he owed her nothing. He'd already been far more thoughtful than she would have expected him to be.

"No, really," she protested with feeling, "I'm fine. We can stay—or you can stay and I can just get a cab to take me home."

But Lukkas shook his head. "I'm going home with the one I brung," he told her.

His grammar had always been impeccable. Had he had too much to drink? But she'd been with him all night and as far as she knew, he'd only had two flutes of champagne. Maybe *she* was the one out of kilter.

"Excuse me?"

"Never mind," he laughed. "It's just an old saying that used to make the rounds a few generations ago."

"What are you, a time traveler?" she asked, thinking of some of the previous remarks he'd made that sounded as if they had come from another era.

"Sometimes," he conceded. "Did you see *One Foot in the Past*?"

He had just mentioned one of her favorite movies. "Yes, I did. That one really made you think," she told him.

Lukkas grinned with genuine pleasure. "I'm beginning to like you more and more with every passing hour, Hanna." He looked as if he was only half kidding.

Don't get carried away, Yohanna warned herself. He was just going along with the party mood. In any event, she was certain he wouldn't remember any of this on Monday morning.

Still, she thought as he called for his driver, what he'd said to her did have a nice sound to it.

Savoring it for a little while longer wouldn't harm anything.

Chapter Eleven

"Would you like me to come back for you later, Mr. Spader?" the limousine driver asked as Lukkas stepped out of the vehicle and then took Yohanna's hand to help her get out.

Lukkas didn't want to communicate the wrong idea to either his driver or to Yohanna.

"No, Henry. Stay right here. This won't take long," he promised.

Lukkas saw the way his driver eyed him and then slanted a glance toward Yohanna. It was obvious what was going through the man's mind. His driver just assumed that he would be capping off the evening with a dalliance. There was no denying that the woman with him was gorgeous, not to mention approachably tempting.

He knew Henry meant well, but the driver was also wrong. Nothing was about to happen other than his walking Hanna to her door.

Yohanna smiled to herself. "I think your driver expects me to invite you in," she said to Lukkas as he brought her to her door.

He wasn't about to explore that possibility. "I learned a long time ago not to concern myself with what others expect of me. I only need to live up to what *I* expect of me," he told her. They were at her door already. It was time to wrap this up and gracefully take his leave. "Thank you for a very nice evening."

"I should be the one thanking you," Yohanna pointed out. She'd had a really wonderful time.

Yohanna suddenly remembered that she was still in possession of the card he'd given her to buy her outfit. "By the way, here's your credit card back," she said, taking it out of her purse and giving it to him. "I just want you to know that I intend to pay you back for the gown and everything else. Just not all at once," she qualified. The bill had come to a figure that represented six months of regular expenses on her budget.

Lukkas shook his head, dismissing her promise. "You wouldn't have had to buy 'the gown and everything' if I hadn't asked you to accompany me to the premiere, so don't worry about it." He flashed an easy smile at her. "I consider it an investment."

Yohanna caught her lower lip between her teeth, chewing on it as she looked down at her gown. She couldn't have him paying for her clothes. "I don't feel right about this," she told him.

"You might not feel right, but you certainly look right," he heard himself saying, giving voice to the way her appearance was affecting him. "And I appreciate you doing this for me."

He made it sound like a sacrifice on her part when it

was anything but. She couldn't help the smile that rose to her lips. All evening she'd felt like a fairy-tale princess. "All my assignments should be so hard."

Initially, he was just going to bring her to her door and watch her go inside. But he found himself wanting to linger, to stay with her a little longer.

Perhaps even go inside.

But he was afraid of where that might lead, and he wasn't ready to go down that path yet.

And he *definitely* wasn't ready to lose possibly the best assistant he had ever had because of a misstep he felt himself being so tempted to make.

He needed to go.

Now.

"See you Monday," he said, taking a couple of steps back, away from her.

"Monday," Yohanna echoed. Instead of opening her door, she remained exactly where she was, struggling with an urge that had materialized out of nowhere.

She desperately wanted him to kiss her good-night. Just one kiss.

Who are you kidding? You don't want just one kiss, you want more. And "more" is just asking for trouble, you know that.

She had a good thing going here: a job she was quickly growing to love. The worst thing in the world would be to allow a spurt of hormones to ruin that for her.

With effort, she took out her key and unlocked her front door.

A moment later she was closing the door behind her.

She was safe.

Safe from herself.

And never sadder about it than right now.

* * *

Yohanna came to work Monday—as well as all the rest of that week—acting as if there hadn't been a moment there, on her doorstep, when she had ceased to be someone who just worked for Lukkas Spader. She decided to make it a mission in her life to learn as much as she could about the man. There was an underlying sadness that reached out to her. She'd always had an inherent desire to help people heal.

For now, though, she needed to concentrate on getting her job done, which in turn meant helping him get *his* job—the movie—done. And something like that, she was beginning to realize, had a great many moving parts that needed to be attended to.

So for now, she pushed that part of herself, the part that was curious about the man, into the far background and did what she always did whenever she couldn't deal with—or have the time for—her private life: she threw herself into her work.

She organized Lukkas's appointments, revamped his schedule, got in touch with people he had penciled in on his calendar and prioritized his would-be "crises" as they came up.

As a small part of that, she made an effort to learn his favorite foods and took to ordering his lunches and, in some cases, his dinners, as well.

Working diligently, she trained herself to anticipate what Lukkas needed even before he realized he needed it. The upshot of that was that within four short weeks, she had his life running like clockwork. That made her completely indispensable to him.

Unknown to Yohanna, in addition to becoming indispensable to Lukkas, she also became the woman who preoccupied him in unguarded moments.

She also began popping up in his dreams, a fact that both intrigued Lukkas and disturbed him.

The latter reaction was because it made him feel that he was being unfaithful to the wife he'd so adored. When Natalie had died so suddenly, he'd been convinced that his heart would never seek anyone out again. That with the threat of loss moving like a specter in the shadows, he couldn't bear to become involved with another woman since that woman could die and leave him, just as Natalie had.

He could, with some effort, guard his thoughts during his waking hours. But when he was asleep, all bets were off—and all fences were breakable. His thoughts of Hanna would creep in and fanciful scenarios would be constructed that he would never allow when he was awake.

This complicated his life, and Lukkas was trying to cope with that as well as with feelings of guilt while attempting to mount a new production and bring it up to its wobbly feet.

At times it felt as though he was constantly shadow boxing, vanquishing one problem only to have another spring up in its place. On occasion he would consider throwing in the towel—those were the times when Hanna would come through the best.

"Your director's on line one," she told him on a particularly exasperating Tuesday morning, bringing a cordless receiver over to him.

Taking the phone from her, Lukkas frowned slightly. He knew before another word was said that he needed to go back to Arizona to find out what was—and wasn't—going on.

His hand covering the mouthpiece, he said, "Hanna, I'm going to need—"

Nodding, she interjected, "I've already called your pilot. The plane will be gassed up and ready to go within the half hour."

That almost left him speechless. "How long have you been a mind reader?" he finally asked her.

Yohanna didn't let the question go to her head. She didn't read minds; she read body language as well as the particular situation that her subject might be in.

"It comes with the territory," she answered. But she was smiling broadly as she said it.

"Just as long as you do, Hanna, that's all that counts." He made a quick calculation. "I hate to ruin any plans you might have for your evening, but I'm going to need you to—"

She'd anticipated this, as well. "I've got a go bag in the trunk of my car. I just have to get it before we leave for the airstrip."

He could only stare at her. There was no way she could have known that he would be receiving this call from Montelle, his director, nor could she have anticipated what the man would say to him.

"What am I thinking now?" Lukkas challenged, his green eyes narrowing ever so slightly as he looked at her, waiting.

"That's easy." She tried to keep a straight face, but failed within a few moments. Her grin was wide. "You're thinking that you don't know how you got so damn lucky to have found someone like me to anticipate your every need, your every move."

"Not exactly, but close enough," he answered with an amused laugh. "We might have to be there a couple of days. Is that all right with you—or would that be interfering with any plans you have for your evenings?"

"I *have* no plans for my evenings. You have my undivided attention," she assured him. "I signed on for the long haul. This is just all part of that."

He really *had* gotten lucky here, Lukkas thought, looking at her. "Right, but that doesn't mean that you have to be enslaved," he pointed out.

"I'll let you know if I feel as if I've been enslaved. Until then, I believe we have work to do," she reminded him. She pointed to the receiver he was still holding in his hand. "Dirk Montelle is still waiting."

He'd almost forgotten. "Oh, damn."

She went to get her go bag.

It was gratifying to find someone who had as much energy as he had, Lukkas thought a short while later. At the same time, it was also somewhat unsettling. He'd never had anyone match him step for step before. In so many ways, Hanna was the perfect assistant.

He just wished that she wasn't so damn attractive, so *distractingly* attractive, he silently amended, while she was at it. Because once each workday was finally done and they had accomplished—thanks to her—everything he had set out to do, thoughts of Hanna—a civilian Hanna—insisted on creeping into his brain and by her very presence, that caused things to get scrambled in his mind. Things such as priorities—even with Hanna prodding him.

Blocking those kinds of thoughts about her was getting harder to do.

* * *

"How much are you paying to rent this 'town'?" she asked Lukkas as they got out of his rental car. It was more or less a rhetorical question, asked in reaction to the oppressive blast of heat that hit her as she got out of the vehicle.

The dusty, weathered town was standing in for Tombstone for another five weeks. "Tombstone," the town that famously watched history being made and legends being born, did not come cheap.

Lukkas quoted the price he and the company that was behind the tourist attraction had arrived at.

"Enough to keep the locals contented," he added. Anticipating a negative remark from her, he was quick to hedge it. "It might look like a lot on paper, but it's actually a bargain. If we had to have these sets built back on the lot, it would have wound up costing a hell of a lot more than what we are currently paying to rent it," he told her.

That part she was well aware of. Yohanna nodded. "I know. I already ran the figures."

"Of course you did," he quipped. "Do you ever do anything spontaneous?" he asked her.

"Yes." Suppressing a smile, she looked him right in the eye and said, "I applied for this job."

Lukkas inclined his head. "Touché." He turned to the director. "So exactly what's our crisis of the day?"

Dirk Montelle took no pleasure in being the bearer of any sort of negative news. "We're falling behind schedule, and if that keeps up, I'm going to lose our leading lady, who can only give us five more weeks. After that, she's committed to a play they're trying out in LA before taking it out on the road."

Always something, Lukkas thought with an inward sigh. "Any way we can speed things up?"

The director laughed shortly. "I wish. But Maddox fancies himself a method actor. Every scene he's in— and that's practically all of them—he wants to shoot over and over again until *he's* 'satisfied.' See the problem?" Montelle asked, exasperated.

Lukkas dragged a hand through an already unruly mop of hair. His hair insisted on curling in the heat. "I see the problem. What I don't see is a solution without getting someone's feathers ruffled in the process."

Yohanna spoke up suddenly. "Bribery," she volunteered.

Both men turned toward her. "Come again?" Lukkas asked.

"Bribery," she repeated. The idea began to take shape in her mind as she spoke. "Offer Maddox a percentage of the picture if he helps you bring it in on time. Tell him if the movie isn't wrapped by the date that your female lead needs to leave, he doesn't get his piece of the movie. You'd be surprised how many mountains suddenly find they can move when the right amount of money is flashed before them."

Lukkas glanced toward his director.

The latter nodded, pleased with the suggestion. "Might be worth a shot," Montelle agreed.

"Okay, let's do it," Lukkas instructed, then looked at Yohanna. "You want to sit in on this since it's your idea?"

"I think it'll probably go over better with Maddox if he thinks this is something going down just between the guys," she pointed out. "Maddox might be charming on the big screen, but the man is a card-carrying male chauvinist pi—" At the last minute she stopped herself and offered Lukkas a wide smile. "You fill in the blank," she told him.

It was a rather insightful description of the man, Lukkas thought. "Someday, you're going to have to tell me where you picked up all this insight on David Maddox," he said.

The smile on her lips turned enigmatic. "I do a lot of reading," she replied vaguely.

"Yes, but Maddox's true state of mind is kept pretty secret," he told her.

"In order for there to be a secret between two people," she told Lukkas, "one of the two has to be dead. Otherwise, the secret—*any* secret—has a time limit on it. When that runs out, the secret 'mysteriously' becomes public knowledge."

Hanna was right, he thought. For such a young person, there were times when she displayed a very old mind. He caught himself wondering things about her that had nothing to do with the job she did.

"Tell someone to send Maddox to me," Lukkas instructed.

Yohanna fairly beamed at him. "You got it." With that, she took off.

Instead of finding someone to carry out Lukkas's order, she decided to go in search of the actor herself. It took a bit of doing, but she finally found the man sequestered in his spacious trailer.

The actor wasn't alone.

One of the continuity girls was with him. A tray with two full plates sat on the table, but neither party seemed to notice the food. Maddox appeared to be on the verge of seducing a not-so-legal young woman.

That was all the production needed. To be shut down

while charges of seducing a minor were brought up against the actor. It had been known to happen, and that sort of Pandora's box, once opened, couldn't be shut again.

"What are you doing in here?" Maddox demanded angrily when he saw her entering his trailer. He waved his hand at her as if he were brushing aside an annoying insect. "Never mind. I don't care. Just get the hell out."

Yohanna stubbornly ignored the actor. Her attention was completely focused on the young girl instead. "How old are you, Rachel?"

The girl seemed surprised, then immediately became defensive. "How do you know my name?"

"I made it a point to learn everyone's name in the crew," Yohanna replied calmly. "Just like Lukkas Spader does. Now answer the question, please. How old are you?" She already knew the answer to that, but she wanted to see what the girl would say.

"I'm nineteen," Rachel informed her with a toss of her head.

"It seems odd that someone who is in charge of making sure the props are exactly in the same place from one take to the next within a scene can't recall what's written down on her own birth certificate."

Rachel's eyes widened to their maximum capacity. "You've seen my birth certificate?" she asked in confusion.

"Everyone working on this movie set is vetted," Yohanna informed her. "From the guy who delivers the bottled water every other day right on up to the director—as well as the actors and actresses," she concluded, looking pointedly at Maddox.

"I will be eighteen—in another month," Rachel declared nervously, her bravado crumbling.

The next moment, scrambling, she gathered up her shoes and the few items of clothing that had already come off. Clutching them to her, Rachel rushed out of the trailer, leaving the door wide-open because both her hands were wrapped around her clothes.

"I hope you're satisfied," Maddox growled angrily. "You've ruined my morning."

"But I saved hers, so it all balances out in the end," she told the actor glibly.

Getting to his feet, Maddox towered over her by almost a foot. The scowl on his face was practically shooting thunderbolts. "I can have your job," he threatened.

She was not about to be intimidated by a man who tried to take advantage of a naive teenager. "If you can do it any better than I can, you're welcome to it, Mr. Maddox."

His scowl intensified. "You think you have such a smart mouth—"

"No, I don't," she interjected. "What I do have, however, is a smart brain. A brain that tells me if you don't take Mr. Spader up on his offer to generously give you a piece of the film, you are going to be taken to court for a breach of contract—and that's just the beginning.

"People like and respect Mr. Spader. You, however, have a reputation as an impossible actor to work with. If you don't get your act together and start promoting some goodwill, you'll wake up one morning to find that your career is over before you ever hit your prime. And because of your rather lavish lifestyle, which I'm sure you're not prepared to curtail, you'll be in debt before you know it with no way to get back on your feet. This isn't conjecture, this is a sure thing."

She could tell he was having trouble following what she was saying. She didn't know how to spell it out for him any better than she'd already done. Lukkas was a lot better at dealing with narcissistic walking egos than she was.

"Do yourself a favor," she told Maddox. "Learn how to get along with people."

"That's what I was doing with that continuity girl before you scared her away. Getting along," he told her with a leer.

Yohanna didn't trust herself to reply to the actor's ridiculous statement. Instead, she simply urged, "Go talk to Mr. Spader and see if you can't fix things by making 'nice' with the man—"

Muttering contemptuously under his breath, Maddox was out of his trailer before she had a chance to finish her sentence.

Chapter Twelve

With Maddox gone and presumably on his way back to the set, Yohanna was about to walk out of the trailer herself. She stopped just short of the doorway when she thought she heard the actor talking to someone who was right outside the trailer door.

If she came out of the man's trailer just now it might create an awkward scene, so she remained where she was, waiting for Maddox and whoever the actor was talking to, to leave.

Standing there, it was impossible not to listen. After a second she realized that the other voice belonged to Lukkas. Her boss had probably gotten tired of waiting for someone to bring Maddox to him so he had gone to look for the actor himself.

That still didn't change her feeling that coming out of Maddox's trailer at this point would be awkward, so she continued to wait where she was as patiently as she could until the two men stopped talking.

It wasn't long.

Maddox's last remark to Lukkas made her think the actor was heading back to the set and back to work. Score one for Lukkas.

Yohanna decided that the best thing to do was to give herself to the count of five before descending the trailer steps and heading back to the set.

Counting off the numbers in her head, she'd gotten up to four when she heard Lukkas raise his voice and say, "You can come out now. Unless, of course, you want to continue playing hide-and-seek."

Yohanna came out instantly. "How did you know I was here?" she asked as she made her way down the steps. Since he was right there at the bottom step, she was all but toe-to-toe with Lukkas.

"Easy. Maddox looked as if he was a hurricane sur-vivor. The only hurricane I know of in the area is you," Lukkas replied. "And I heard what you said to him in the trailer—the door was left open," he pointed out in case she'd forgotten. "Nice job. You went a little off book," he told her, since she *had* strayed from his initial message. "But in general you've got good instincts."

What had surprised him most of all when he'd listened to her talking to the actor was that she hadn't fawned over the man the way almost everyone else on the set did. "Someone else would have been intimidated by Mad-dox's fame and personality—"

"I don't like people who abuse their positions—or use it to seduce young, impressionable girls," she added with a frown. She had a feeling that even if Rachel had been underage and the actor had known it, it wouldn't have made any difference to him.

He grinned as he walked back to the center of the set with Hanna. "I kind of got that impression when you read Maddox the riot act."

"No riot act," she denied calmly. "I just gave the man a glimpse of his future if he didn't get his act together and change—like, *immediately*."

Lukkas was having trouble hiding his amusement. The woman was feisty—and he found that to be very attractive. Just like the rest of her.

"So now you're the ghost of things to come in the future?" he asked.

"No, just somebody trying to do her job as best she can."

"Well, I'd say that you've succeeded admirably well," he told her—and then enumerated what she'd accomplished in a relatively short amount of time. "Thanks to you, Rachel's virtue will remain intact—for at least a little while longer—and this film just might get made on time after all." He spared her a rather long, thoughtful look. He couldn't help thinking that he'd gotten lucky all because of an off-chance remark he'd made to Theresa.

"After we wrap up tonight, I'd like to buy you dinner to show you my gratitude." The restaurant in town served good, decent food, but he knew of an excellent restaurant in the next city that served the kind of prime rib that most men only dreamed about.

Yohanna shook her head. "You don't have to do that," she told him.

"You turned Maddox into a human being. Who knows how long that'll last, but I learned in this business to take everything as it comes because things might just fall apart tomorrow. Anyway, after this transformation act with Maddox, it's the least I can do." He stopped short of the perimeter of the town. "I'm not taking no for an answer," he informed her.

"Then I'd better not give it," she replied.

"Smart," he commented. "Now let's get back to work." And with that, he walked into the town with Hanna right beside him.

He was getting very used to that.

It occurred to her as she watched Lukkas in action on the set later that day that the producer was involved in every single facet of the movie. He not only put himself out there to mediate disputes between crew members as well as between the people in the cast when tempers grew short or egos clashed, but Lukkas also made sure he had his finger in every single pie on the set.

Nothing was too large for him to tackle or too small to escape his notice.

Although she considered herself an unharnessed dynamo, just watching Lukkas work made her feel downright exhausted.

But eventually, several would-be crises later, the day finally did come to a close—later than she'd anticipated but still early enough to be within the parameters of the same day.

There were two and a half hours left until midnight as she went to Lukkas's trailer to check for any last-minute instructions he might have for her for the following day.

"There're *always* instructions for the next day," he told her. "But they can wait until morning." He powered down his laptop and closed the cover with finality. "Ready for that dinner I promised you?" Lukkas asked.

She'd thought that he'd forgotten. Stifling a yawn, Yohanna said, "I've been watching you all day. Toward the end, you looked as if you could barely put one foot in front of the other. You need to get some sleep," she advised. "You can buy me dinner some other time."

"Very little placing one foot in front of the other is involved in eating dinner," he quipped. "Another lesson I learned some time ago is do whatever you're planning on doing *now*. There might not be a tomorrow no matter how well you plan for it." There was sadness in his eyes as he added, "So why not celebrate each day as you can before the opportunity is gone?"

He was thinking of his wife, Yohanna thought, wishing there was something she could do to reduce that sadness. But she knew that wasn't possible. Everyone had to work their grief out on their own. The best she could do was to be silently supportive.

Offering him a smile, she said, "I just thought you might be kind of tired after being a superhero all day."

His brow furrowed slightly, the way it did when he was trying to figure something out. "I'm afraid I don't get the reference," Lukkas confessed. "How am I a superhero?"

She enumerated the ways. "Having the patience of Job. Tackling one problem after another. Getting people what they want—"

"When it's possible," he reminded her.

He was the one who decided what could be done and what couldn't. Had they really been in Tombstone, he would have been the marshal of the town, she thought. "You make it possible."

He laughed, shaking his head. "Not that what you're saying isn't really great for my ego, but you're going to have to tone down your image of me just a little. You make it sound as if I have the power of life and death over this little mobile community. You know I don't."

"Figuratively, then," she conceded. The next moment she tried to make him understand just where she was coming from. She figured that she'd observed him long enough to make this kind of judgment call. "Just telling it the way it is. And the way it is, Lukkas, is that you're one of the good guys." She told him in all seriousness, "The world needs more good guys."

He waved off the compliment. "Well, I don't know about the world," he said wryly, "but right now, I need to get something to eat before I start gnawing on the trees around here. So how about it?" he asked, looking at her. "Join me for dinner?"

She didn't like eating alone and she *did* like his company. She had no real reason to beg off. But the thought of driving to the next town—which wasn't all *that* close—was daunting.

"As long as we get something to eat here," she told him. "Because you might be ready to go another round or so, but I'm pretty beat."

"*Here* it is, then," he responded.

As it turned out, the building designated to serve as the local brothel in the movie was actually a restaurant geared to feed the tourists who came through the town seeking local color. It was also where the cast and crew ate their meals.

"Nothing fancy," he told her. "But if you want to stay in town, it's not half-bad."

"Is that your version of a rave review?" she asked, amused at his choice of words.

"No, that's my version of being honest. I'd rather drive

to Scottsdale, but it *is* a bit of a drive, and in the interest of not falling asleep behind the wheel—" he looked at her significantly since he had a feeling that had been her reasoning for remaining in the immediate area "—I thought this was a good alternative."

Yohanna recalled some of the recent reading she'd been doing on life back in Wyatt Earp's time. "Please tell me the restaurant isn't called Big Nose Kate's."

Lukkas laughed. "No, that's the name of the brothel in the movie. I don't know what the restaurant is actually called," he confessed. "Only that so far no one's been rushed to the hospital yet."

"Always a heartening piece of information to know," she conceded.

As it turned out, the restaurant specialized in Mexican cuisine and had several things on the menu that looked appealing to her. She finally decided to get the enchilada ranchero.

"Make that two," Lukkas told the young waitress as he handed her his menu, as well.

The young woman smiled as she looked from him to Yohanna. "Good choice. It's my favorite, too. I'll be right back with your bread," the waitress promised as she withdrew.

Lukkas leaned over in the booth to tell her, "Dirk Montelle wanted me to tell you thanks."

"For?" Yohanna asked.

She couldn't think of a reason why the director would want to thank her for anything. She'd had very few dealings with the director since she and Lukkas had arrived in Arizona this time around.

"Well, Montelle seems to think that you're the reason Maddox is behaving. Maddox is actually satisfied after only a couple of takes of each scene instead of his usual ten or twelve takes. Montelle told me that whatever spell you cast on Maddox, he hopes it's a long-lasting one. According to him, his ulcer has stopped acting up." Lukkas grinned at her. "You might have a career in medicine ahead of you."

She was flattered, but she didn't believe in taking credit when none was due. "You overheard what I said to Maddox. I just played on his insecurities. That wasn't magic. It was just using common sense, that's all."

"I agree," he told her. "But most people…well, they'd rather believe a little hocus pocus was involved. If you took a poll, I think you'd find out that people like believing that something more powerful than them is watching over the world, making things right." He smiled at her. "It makes them feel safer," he told her.

Before Yohanna had a chance to protest again, the waitress returned with the bread and several pats of butter, just as she'd promised. She carried it in on a wooden cutting board and placed it in front of Lukkas.

"I'll be back soon with your orders," she told them before once more retreating into the background.

Lukkas looked at the bread. It was situated in the middle of the cutting board. A sharp knife was next to it. "I guess she wants me to do the honors," he said, picking up the knife.

"I can do that if you like," Yohanna was quick to offer, thinking that perhaps he'd just subtly indicated that he'd rather not do the cutting.

"Not that I don't appreciate the fact that you keep trying to jump in and take care of practically all the details that infiltrate my daily existence, Hanna, but I actually am capable of cutting my own bread," he assured her good-naturedly.

"I never meant for you to think that I thought that you couldn't," she told him.

He surprised her by laughing out loud at her statement.

"Now, *that's* confusing, even without any wine to dull the brain," he joked. "By the way, I'm not offended, I'm amused. I might not have the thickest skin around, but it's definitely thicker than tissue paper," he assured her.

Cutting two thick slices of the warm bread, Lukkas gave her the first piece and took the second one for himself. When she didn't immediately pick up her piece from her bread plate, he nodded at it, saying, "You have to eat it while it's still warm."

"It's bread. How much of a difference can it make?" she asked, dutifully breaking off a piece of her slice and popping it into her mouth.

The instant the bread touched her tongue, she found herself smiling. There was something comforting about consuming the warm slice.

"You're right," she told him.

"It does happen every once in a while," he told her with a conspiratorial wink.

The restaurant was dimly lit. It was also rather noisy and fairly filled with people. Yet when she found herself on the receiving end of Lukkas's wink, she felt as if they were the only two people in the entire place.

With very little effort, her imagination could run away with her.

Don't get carried away. He's just being himself, nothing personal, she silently insisted.

Yohanna struggled to rechannel her thoughts.

"How did you find this place?" she asked him. "This town," she amended. "For the movie, I mean."

Great. You keep talking and you'll really convince him that you're a blithering idiot.

"The usual way," he told her. Then, seeing that she was still at a loss as to what had happened, he elaborated, "I sent out my location scout. Hank usually knows just what I have in mind and he's pretty good about nailing down what I'm looking for.

"We were lucky this place was here," he admitted. "But even if it hadn't been, I would have had sets built on the studio's back lot. With the wonder of CGI available these days, almost anything can be dressed up to look like what you have in mind."

She saw a basic contradiction in that. "If that's what you think, why bother with a location scout?" She would have thought that going with computer-generated imagery first would eliminate the hunt for a perfect location.

Her question brought a smile to his lips. "Because like a lot of people, I like the real thing rather than having to deal with a fake—or worse, dealing with nothing at all, having to pretend that it's there. A lot of actors don't act so much as they 'react.' Having an actual location helps them with that part," he concluded. "Make sense?"

She nodded. "Yes."

He could see right through her. "You'd say that even if it didn't, wouldn't you?"

"I'm not on the clock right now," she reminded him. "I don't have to answer that."

He grinned. Her nonanswer *was* an answer. "You just did," he told her.

Ignoring that, she took a different direction. "Why this story? This picture?"

"Why all these questions?" he asked. "Are you planning on putting out a book about working on this film after we wrap up?"

"You mean like an exposé?" she asked.

"That's exactly what I mean." Had he misjudged her? Was she someone who ultimately gave her allegiance to the man or woman on top, everyone else be damned?

He didn't like entertaining that thought.

"I'm just being curious, that's all," Yohanna admitted. "If you don't want to answer my question, that's okay."

"Who said I didn't want to answer?" he asked. "I was just curious why you wanted to know, that's all. But to answer your question, I've always loved Westerns—what little boy growing up in Texas doesn't?" he challenged, prepared to listen if Yohanna had a contradictory piece of information. But she didn't. If anything, she looked as if she agreed with him. "Anyway, I had so much fun making my first Western a couple of years ago, I decided to do it again."

"Hoping that lightning will strike again?"

It was a referral to the fact that he had won his first film award for the Western he'd just mentioned.

"I'd be lying if I said that it hadn't crossed my mind. But I'm not backing this movie because I'm actively hoping for another award or even another nomination. I'm making this film because I like the story and I believe it'll make a good movie.

"Besides, I really do enjoy the whole process, every step of the way. Especially when I have someone exceedingly competent I can rely on working for me." He could see that her inherent modesty wasn't allowing her to realize he was referring to her.

"In case I'm being too vague about the matter, I'm talking about you, Hanna," he told her, and then got a kick out of the surprised expression on her face. "You're a godsend and I intend to send Theresa Manetti *all* my catering business from here on in."

She'd already made the connection between Cecilia and Theresa. As far as she was concerned, she owed the latter a debt herself. "I'm sure that'll make her very happy."

Seeing that the waitress was heading in their direction with a large tray, Yohanna quickly cleared the table, stacking the small bread plates on the cutting board. The waitress arrived at their table and distributed the two plates. Since their orders were identical, there was no effort necessary to match the customer with the proper order.

The young woman looked from Lukkas to the woman sitting opposite him.

"Please be careful when you're touching the plates. They're very hot. Should you burn your hand anyway, just ask for me. I've always got something with me to take the pain away."

"Prescription drugs?" he asked, not quite able to cast her in the role of someone who distributed drugs, however innocuously.

"Over-the-counter spray," she corrected. "Where would I get prescription drugs?" she asked.

"No clue," he answered, and then confessed, "That was just a wild guess on my part."

Yohanna focused on the conversation. She'd first thought of Lukkas as being exceedingly closemouthed, but she now realized that he only spoke to someone on a regular basis if he considered that person worth the effort.

She promised herself that he would *always* find her worth the effort he put in.

Chapter Thirteen

"I want you to know that I appreciate everything that you've done."

They were halfway through the meal when, out of the blue, Lukkas said that to her.

Yohanna felt her nerves kick up a notch.

This was the way her last boss had begun the last conversation they'd ever had, the one about how her position had been terminated—as had she.

Taking a deep breath, she told herself that this time around she wasn't going to just be a stunned victim who disappeared quietly. This time, if she was being terminated, she would go on her own terms and with dignity.

"But…?" she challenged, waiting for the second shoe—or cowboy boot in this case—to fall.

"But?" Lukkas repeated quizzically, as if he had no idea where the word was coming from.

"Yes, but…" Since he still wasn't saying anything, she filled in the blanks for him. "You've been very happy with my work, but now I have to go."

"You do?" he asked, clearly confused since this was apparently the first time he'd heard this. "Is it something I did?"

Yohanna stared at him. Why was he toying with her? That wasn't like the man she'd come to know.

"Well, yes. You're the one terminating me."

Caught completely off guard, he put down his knife and fork. "Wait—what? I know I made a movie about parallel universes, but I really don't believe in them and I *know* I didn't just terminate you in this life."

Now it was her turn to be confused. "Weren't you just leading up to that? You've been happy with my work up until now, but since I did such a good job organizing things for you, you're all set and no longer need my services."

Lukkas slowly shook his head, as if to clear it of cobwebs. "Unless I'm a victim of some kind of new strain of amnesia, I didn't say any of that."

"Yes, you did," she insisted, and then conceded, "Okay, maybe not in so many words—"

"Not in any words," Lukkas told her, cutting in.

A glimmer of hope began to raise its head. "Then, what *were* you saying?" she asked.

She was partially relieved and yet afraid to go that route in case her premonition turned out to be right. She'd been blindsided once and it had really upset her, but this time around, it would do more than that. It would hurt.

Badly.

"I thought I said it," Lukkas told her. Since there was

a difference of opinion on that, he relented and said, "Well, at least part of it."

"Say it again—" Yohanna urged. "So we're both clear on it."

He paused for a moment, as if recreating the moment for himself. "I said that I just wanted you to know that I appreciate everything that you've done."

She waited. When there was no follow-up, she asked. "And that was it?"

"No," he admitted.

Okay, here it came, she thought. "Okay, go ahead," she urged, resigned to having the next words turn out not to her liking.

"I was going to say that I knew talk, even praise, was cheap and I wanted to show you that I was sincere by offering you a raise."

"A raise?" It took effort to keep her jaw from dropping into her lap. "As in money?" she asked him, rather stunned.

"No, a raise as in my levitating you. Yes, of course, as in money," he told her. "Like it or not, money's the fastest way of communicating approval and pleasure, just like withholding it communicates disapproval. The latter, by the way, has nothing to do with you," he assured her.

With the threat of her just walking out on him over, he resumed eating. "When Janice—your predecessor— left, I was certain I was never going to find anyone to take her place. She was *that* good.

"You, however, not only took her place," he continued, "you have surpassed her, something I never thought would be humanly possible. Janice was on top of *everything*, handling things as they came up. You seem to be able to anticipate what's going to happen, and you do it all effortlessly.

"I just wanted you to know that I might not say anything at the time, but I'm aware of what you're doing and I'm really very impressed with it all. The raise is my way of trying to keep you."

"Keep me?" Did he think she was going to leave? Where had he gotten *that* idea? "I'm not about to go anywhere," she assured him. "I really like this job." When she'd taken it, she hadn't realized just how much she *would* like it.

"Word's going to get out about your efficiency and your effortless juggling act," he told her. It would be just a matter of time before it happened—that much he knew. "There'll be people who will try to steal you away from me by making you lucrative offers and upping the ante. I just want you to promise me that when that happens, not if, but *when*—" he stopped her before she could argue the point "—you'll come to me and give me a chance to match the offer—or top it," he added, thinking that might be more of an incentive to make her remain in his employ.

His eyes pinned hers and he asked, "So do we have a deal?"

She put her hand out to him to seal the bargain. "Absolutely," she promised as Lukkas took her hand and shook it directly over what was left on their plates. "But I think you're talking about something that isn't going to happen."

His opinion differed from hers—and he had experience on his side. "This is a very cutthroat business, Hanna. You'd be surprised what people are capable of just to get slightly ahead of the 'other guy.' Just remember, if there's anything I can do to make things easier for you, all you have to do is tell me."

"Well, there is one thing I can think of right off the bat," she told him, her expression solemn and giving nothing away.

"Name it," he urged.

Her mouth began to show just the slightest hint of a curve. "You could let go of my hand," she told him. "I need it to cut into the second enchilada."

Embarrassed, he flushed. "Oh, sorry."

Her hand had felt so right in his that just for a moment, he'd forgotten he was holding it. The second she said something, he realized he was holding on to her hand like some love-smitten fool and he immediately let it go.

He was reacting to Hanna.

Reacting to her not as an incredibly capable assistant—and quite simply the answer to his prayers—but as a woman.

It had been unconscious on his part.

He had ceased to think of himself as a man, with a man's basic needs, the moment he'd heard of his wife's death. He had been convinced then—and now—that that part of him had shut down, completely and irrevocably, and somewhere along the line, that part of him had just withered away and died.

In his work he was constantly surrounded by countless attractive women of all ages, many of whom thought nothing of using their physical attributes to get ahead.

That sort of thing didn't work with him. He hadn't been tempted, not even one single time. He saw them, noted the "special" assets they brought to the interaction and felt absolutely *nothing*. There hadn't even been any latent stirrings.

For almost three years now he'd viewed situations and women in his capacity as a producer, as someone who knew the benefit of giving the public what they wanted—and the public *always* wanted a young, sexy actress to look at.

But as far as that being something that *he* wanted for himself? That never once even entered into the picture. He felt he was no longer attracted *that* way to women, no matter how sexy or how beautiful.

Until Hanna had come into his life.

Because this live wire of a woman *did* stir things within him that had nothing to do with producing a movie, nothing to do with the hectic agenda he maintained, and everything to do with the inner man he'd just assumed had atrophied from grief.

He was making this pitch to keep her faithful to his company—in effect, to him—because in addition to seeing her as an asset of the highest quality, he simply didn't want to lose *her.* Not just the dynamo of an assistant, not the woman who could keep all those balls successfully in the air, but he didn't want to lose Hanna. Period.

Feeling that way scared the hell out of him for so many reasons. It scared him because he knew what happened when a person became attached to another human being. That sort of a connection left him open to a world of pain if that association should terminate—abruptly or otherwise—for any of a number of reasons.

There was also the problem of guilt.

Guilt because he was going on with his life and Natalie no longer had a life to go on with. Having feelings for someone other than his wife seemed somehow unfaithful, disloyal to her memory.

Natalie deserved better than that.

"Is everything all right?" Yohanna asked him.

Lukkas roused himself and did his best to look as if he hadn't been miles away, lost in thought just now.

"Yes. Why?"

She shrugged, as if she thought perhaps she *had* been overreacting. "You had this very faraway look on your face just now."

"Just thinking about tomorrow's filming," he lied smoothly. Or so he thought.

"Tomorrow's filming," Yohanna repeated, then recited the latest schedule for filming the day after Halloween. "They're doing scene sixteen and scene thirty and the assistant director is doing some secondary background shots of the corral where the gunfight is supposed to take place."

Lukkas could only shake his head in wonder, not to mention in complete admiration. "Like I said, you're absolutely amazing."

She hardly heard the compliment, honing in on the sadness she'd glimpsed in his eyes for an unguarded moment just a minute ago. She was willing to bet that Lukkas hadn't even remotely been thinking about the next day's shooting schedule. Something else was on his mind, something far more personal.

"Listen," she began haltingly, "I might be out of line here…"

"Go on," he told her quietly.

She took another breath, wondering if she shouldn't have said anything, then decided it wasn't in her to turn a blind eye to someone else's pain—especially if that someone else mattered to her as much as Lukkas did.

"But if you ever…you know, need to talk to someone about…anything," she finally said, "I'm a pretty good listener." And then she added with what she hoped was a convincing smile, "Two ears, no waiting."

Not that he planned to tell her anything, but it was nice to know someone cared enough to offer help of a sort.

"I appreciate the offer," he told her. "But the fastest way to lose a friend is to burden them with having to listen to someone go on about things that don't matter to anyone else but them."

"Funny, I was thinking just the opposite," Yohanna told him. "Sharing concerns, things that worry you, that's the ultimate sign of trust, not to mention that something like that promotes bonding."

"Okay, I'll keep that in mind," he told her. Finished with his meal, he set his knife and fork down on his empty plate.

"And in case you forgot this part, it works two ways," he pointed out. "If you ever need to unload, say, about a boyfriend who feels as if you're spending way too much time at work," he elaborated with a smile, "I'm here."

"I wouldn't hold my breath if I were you," she advised.

"You don't believe in complaining?" he asked, curious.

"It's not that," she told him. "I don't have anything to complain about, at least, not in that department."

He took a sip of water to clear his throat. "Let me guess, your boyfriend's perfect?"

"My 'boyfriend' is nonexistent," Yohanna corrected glibly.

Lukkas looked at her, rather surprised. When she'd first come to work for him, she'd said there was no boyfriend in her life. He'd just assumed, as the weeks went by, that that was no longer the case. To find out that he'd assumed incorrectly…well, that pleased him. Pleased him a great deal.

"You don't have a boyfriend?" he asked with an air of disbelief.

Yohanna closed her eyes for a second, desperately trying to ward off a feeling of déjà vu.

"Please don't sound like my mother," she all but begged. "That's her recurring theme. Except that she says that exact same sentence in a much higher voice— almost a screech. That's usually followed by her telling me that her best friend's dermatologist's cousin's son is going to be calling me and I should say yes when he asks me out because, after all, I'm not getting any younger."

Lukkas didn't bother trying to stifle his laugh. "That's very funny."

"Not when you're on the receiving end of the conversation. Trust me on that," she added with more than a little feeling.

Lukkas stopped laughing and looked at her in surprise. "You're serious?"

She nodded. "I only wish I wasn't. I think my mother had posters made up of my high school graduation picture with the caption 'Please date me' written across the bottom. The only saving grace is that the last line has a disclaimer that reads 'Serial killers need not apply.'

"My mother *really* wants grandchildren," Yohanna explained. "All her friends have at least one, if not more. My mother desperately wants to be able to brag about a granddaughter or grandson." There was pity in her voice as she continued, "She feels I've failed her—and she makes sure that I'm aware of that every time she calls me."

As if aware of what she was saying—and to whom—

Yohanna raised her eyes to his. "Wait, how did my offer to be your sounding board turn into my crying on your shoulder?" Embarrassed and aware that she had crossed a line, Yohanna flushed. "I'm sorry. I'm not really sure what just happened here."

He didn't want her to feel embarrassed. If anything, Lukkas felt touched that she'd let him into her world. "Easy. You needed someone to talk to and I just said something to trigger the release. Don't worry about it," he assured her. "As a matter of fact, I kind of like the fact that you felt you could confide in me." When she rolled her eyes in response, he went a step further. "No, really. I think I needed that to remind me just how good I have it."

Glancing down at the table, Lukkas saw that she had finished her meal. That made two of them.

"Would you like any dessert?" he asked and then of-fered, "I can have the waitress bring back the menu."

"I would *love* dessert," Yohanna responded with feel-ing, then quickly held up her hand to stop him from wav-ing over their waitress. "But I'd have to wear it. I'm so full, I couldn't fit in another bite—really," she protested.

"Are you sure?" he asked. "We could get it to go." Lukkas saw an impish smile, which totally charmed him. He wondered if she knew that when she smiled like that, she was really hard to resist. "What?"

"I could have it for breakfast." She realized she prob-ably wasn't making any sense to him, so she elaborated, "When I was a kid, I always thought having cake for breakfast was a dream come true. My mother, of course, had other thoughts on the matter. Not to mention that she was very militant about not consuming too much sugar or too many calories. She told me that no man would want to marry me if I looked like the Goodyear Blimp.

"What are you doing?" she asked when he raised his hand to catch the waitress's eye.

"Making a dream come true," he told her simply. "And also asking for the check."

When the waitress came to their table a couple of minutes later he said to her, "We'd like to see the dessert menu, please."

"Right away." The waitress plucked a menu from one of the other waitresses walking by. The other woman was carrying several to the reservation desk.

When she offered the menu to Lukkas, he nodded at Hanna. "It's for her."

"No, really—" Yohanna began to beg off, waving away the menu.

"What kind of cake do you have?" he asked the waitress.

She rattled off four different kinds. When she came to vanilla with pecan sauce, Lukkas noticed a spark in Hanna's eyes. He had his answer.

"She'll take that one," he told the waitress. "Make it to go. Wait, make that two slices to go," Lukkas amended. He saw the quizzical way Hanna looked at him. "Hey, I like cake, too."

"You really didn't have to do that," Yohanna told him after the waitress left to prepare the desserts for transport.

"Sure I did," he argued amicably. "After all, how often does a man get a chance to make a little girl's dream come true?"

She had no answer for that. She could only smile. She was seriously beginning to understand that if there was one thing that Lukkas Spader could do, it was make dreams come true.

For big girls as well as for little ones.

Chapter Fourteen

Lukkas didn't need to look at a calendar.

He knew.

The very date had been burned into his brain, into his heart, since that horrible day three years ago.

Three years.

One thousand ninety-five days ago, his world had ended.

Part of him had desperately hoped that he would find a way to just move on, to block the numbing feelings of loss out of his awareness. For the most part, he'd succeeded.

There were whole chunks of time that he could function without those horrific feelings suddenly ambushing him, destroying everything in its path but the terrible memory of those first few hours, those first few days, where nothing, especially his existence, made any sense.

Those first few days when he couldn't quite understand how he could go on breathing in a world without Natalie in it.

As time went by, the ambushes occurred less frequently. He found a way to function, to be useful. To even continue building his career.

But on the anniversary of his wife's death, it had all come crashing back with a vengeance that first year—and then again the second year.

This year was no exception.

Lukkas could feel himself shutting down even as he struggled not to let it happen.

This year, in an attempt to keep his feelings of loss at bay, Lukkas completely surrounded himself with work—or thought he did.

But because of Yohanna's efficiency, everything was moving so smoothly, he didn't even need to be out on location at this moment. Wasn't really needed anywhere.

Without these artificial roadblocks in place, the grief easily found him.

That morning, Yohanna saw the difference in Lukkas's deportment immediately. There had always been that slight hint of sadness in his eyes. She'd noticed it the very first day when she had interviewed for her job. However, it had been subdued. Today, that aura of sadness seemed to have created some sort of invisible, impenetrable force field around him.

Lukkas was unapproachable and, while not short-tempered, noticeably short with those around him. Including her.

Trying to get to the bottom of the cause, Yohanna waited until she knew he'd be alone in his trailer to broach the subject. Even as she told herself that she should just let things slide, she still found herself going to his trailer and knocking on his door.

She had to knock twice before she heard any response from within. At least, she *thought* she'd heard something, but it could have just been the noise coming from the set.

Taking a deep breath, she tried the door. It wasn't locked.

Because she'd ventured this far, she decided to let herself in.

"Lukkas?"

There was no answer.

Thinking that perhaps he hadn't heard her, she made her way to the rear of the trailer, to the area that had been converted into his bedroom.

That was where she found him.

Lukkas was packing the suitcase he'd brought with him on the plane.

Surprised, Yohanna could only surmise they were flying back to California.

"Are we leaving?" It was the first thing she could think to ask.

Completely involved in his own heartache, Lukkas hadn't heard her come in until she'd spoken. His nerves were very close to the surface and he jumped.

"Don't you knock?" he demanded.

She had never seen him uptight or angry before. The image was unsettling.

"I did. I thought that maybe you hadn't heard me so I tried the door. You didn't lock it."

"And so you thought you'd just waltz right in." It was an accusation more than a statement of fact. An annoyed accusation.

"I think that's self-evident," she responded politely.

Indicating the open suitcase, she asked again, "Are we going back to the studio?"

"I am." His tone made it apparent that he completely excluded her from this.

Yohanna asked, "What about me?"

Lukkas shrugged. "You can do whatever you want to do," he declared, biting the words off.

He wasn't even looking at her, just addressing his words to the contents of his suitcase. But why was he so angry at her? What had she done to bring about such a drastic change?

Yohanna vacillated between just quietly withdrawing and remaining in the trailer for what was shaping up to be some sort of a confrontation.

Tempted, she almost went with the first option. But if she did, she knew that this raw feeling would always be there between them should she somehow still wind up staying in his employ.

For her own peace of mind, she needed to clear this up, whatever "this" was. "Did I do something wrong?" she asked.

He swung around to look at her. "No. You're perfect. Absolutely perfect," he snapped.

"If I'm so perfect, then why are you biting off my head and acting as if you're angry at the whole world— me in particular?"

"Maybe because I am angry at the whole world," he retorted.

Yohanna noticed that he hadn't singled her out the way she had. She became more determined to find out what was going on.

"Because…?"

"Because!" he shouted, slamming down the lid of his

suitcase. He did it so hard, the suitcase fell off the bed. The contents flew out all over the floor.

Yohanna automatically moved to pick up his clothes for him and Lukkas grabbed her by the shoulder, pulling her up.

"Don't!" he ordered gruffly.

At that moment he saw his reflection in the mirror hanging over his bureau, saw the anger that all but distorted his face.

The sight was so startling it abruptly knocked the air out of him.

Dropping his hand to his side, he murmured, "I'm sorry," to her. And then, in a stronger voice, he reinforced his apology. "I'm really sorry. I have no right to take this out on you."

Because he'd apologized, she immediately forgave him. He appeared genuinely sorry and that only made her more determined than ever to find out what was going on. She had spent too much time in Lukkas's company to believe that this was his true nature and the rest had just been a ruse.

Something had gotten to him in a way that she didn't think anything could. Something that seemed to completely shatter him.

And then, suddenly, it hit her. She knew what had caused this transformation.

"Talk to me, Lukkas," she urged him. "Please."

He didn't want to talk, to think, to in any way peel back the layers and make this any worse than it already was.

He tried to make her leave. "Look, I've done enough to you. Please, just go—"

"No," she answered. With that, she planted herself on

the edge of the bed, where she intended to remain until she got him to unload. "I'm not going anywhere. You need to get this out, to talk this through. Lukkas, you really need to get those feelings out before they wind up eating you alive."

Lukkas said nothing as he looked at her, but she could almost feel him struggling with himself.

"I'll start you off," she offered, then quietly continued, "This has to do with your late wife, doesn't it?"

The stricken expression in Lukkas's eyes told her she had guessed correctly.

"What set you off?" she asked. "Did you come across something of hers you'd forgotten was there or—?"

"The accident was today," he said hoarsely, his voice distant, as if he could somehow separate himself from the words he was saying.

Yohanna recalled the article she'd glimpsed on her tablet. He was talking about the car accident that had ended his wife's life.

Her heart went out to him in empathy.

"Each year after my dad died," she said quietly, "on the anniversary of his passing, I wound up reliving how I felt when I watched him slip away— We were at the hospital with him, my mom and I," she interjected.

She saw fresh grief pass over Lukkas's face.

"Well, I wasn't there when Natalie 'slipped away.' I was busy being the big-shot producer on the set," he told her bitterly. "I was supposed to be there with her, supposed to be the one who drove her to the doctor's office for her appointment—but I was too busy and I forgot all about her appointment. We were having our first baby and I *forgot*," he told her, his self-disdain almost palpable. "So, ever the resourceful wife, she drove herself.

The front tire had a blowout. Natalie plowed into a street-light. She must have been so scared—" His voice broke.

"If you had been with her, the front tire would have still had a blowout," she pointed out. "As horrible as it was, her death wasn't your fault," she insisted. "Stop beating yourself up over it."

Yohanna could see that she just wasn't getting through to him. "From what I can piece together, your wife was a wonderful, kind person. She wouldn't have wanted you to do this to yourself. She would have wanted you to honor her memory by being strong and going on with your life," she told him.

He said nothing, but she saw the unshed tears shimmering in his eyes.

Without fully realizing what she was doing, only motivated by the need to offer comfort, Yohanna rose to her feet and put her arms around him. He tried to shrug her off, but she persisted. Slowly, she felt him stop resisting.

"Let it go so you can heal," she urged softly, hugging him harder, doing her best to break through all the layers he'd thrown up around himself, shutting grief in, shutting compassion out.

She wasn't sure just how long she stood there, offering him solace as best she could.

Nor was she really clear as to who made the next move after that.

Whether it was her—or Lukkas.

Whichever did, one minute she was trying valiantly to give him some of her own strength, the strength she'd built up to help her deal with life after losing the father she adored. The very next moment it was as if some sort of spell had been cast, some sort of floodgate had been opened, because that was when her lips were pressed against his.

She could taste his tears—and his pain. Something within her opened up as well, something that not only could offer comfort in the face of grief, but that actually *drew* comfort from the very act of offering it to someone else.

It progressed at almost a breakneck speed immediately after that.

Wanting only to help give voice to his very real pain and, just maybe, to diminish it and its hold on him by that very act, she discovered that there was a solid ache within her, as well. An ache that craved having some sort of real contact, to touch and be touched by another human being in a way that allowed actual souls to touch.

A real sense of urgency all but throbbed in his veins.

Lukkas slanted his mouth over hers over and over again. Each time he did, the stakes were raised. And so was the promise of a reward.

Lukkas had had no idea how much he really needed this sort of contact, a contact he had denied himself because he'd believed that part of him—the part that could be reached by only a woman's touch—had been snuffed out the day his wife had been killed. To find out that it hadn't, that it was, instead, alive and in need of thriving, both dismayed him and thrilled him. To that end he felt utterly confused but alive for perhaps the first time in three years.

Suddenly very much in need to complete this exotic journey he had started, Lukkas undid buttons, coaxed articles of clothing away from the areas that they covered.

The warm flesh he discovered underneath the banished clothing easily started his pulse racing.

And fed a desire for more.

He ran his hands along Hanna's body, his own responding to it the way he hadn't responded to anyone in so long.

It was not unlike coming out of a deep sleep then becoming aware of limbs that had been all but paralyzed such a short while ago. There was no such paralysis, no such numbness, afflicting him now.

Every part of his body was alive and *feeling* every subtle nuance that being here like this with Hanna had created.

In its grip, Lukkas found himself racing to consummate this feeling, to capture it quickly before it was gone and he returned to the isolated, cold, lonely chamber he had existed in until just now.

Yohanna gave him no resistance.

Just the opposite was true.

She enflamed him, fanning the growing fire he had within him until the flames filled out every single corner of his being, leaving no room for grief or regrets of any kind.

Afraid of losing this feeling, of becoming trapped within his self-created prison once again, Lukkas ceased exploring the subtleties of her body and gave in to the overwhelming desire to unite it with his.

One moment his eyes were on hers, their hands delicately interlaced. The next he was driving himself into her and so creating a union where none had been before.

Ever mindful of her, Lukkas watched her face as he began to move. If for any reason at all, she had changed her mind about this, he'd be able to see it and, as hard as it would be for him, he would stop.

There would be deep regret, but he would stop.

But there was no such sign from her.

Instead, Yohanna instantly matched his rhythm. He stepped up the pace.

So did she.

They rose together at breakneck speed, taking the summit together. His arms tightened around her as the internal fireworks came to a head.

For one brief, shining moment, he felt himself both excited and at peace.

Yohanna kissed him, urgently pressing her mouth against his with every fiber of her being. It was as if she wanted Lukkas to know that whatever might come afterward, in this one moment, they belonged to one another and all was perfect in the tiny universe populated only by the two of them.

Yohanna nestled her body against his. She remained there even as the euphoria began to slip away, withdrawing into the same shadows where it had lay hidden, waiting for just that one opportunity to emerge.

Lukkas slowly became aware of everything.

Of the scent of her hair, of the light, sweet taste that her lips had brought to his, of the softness of her skin as her body remained curled into his.

Everything.

No doubt sensing the lull in what they'd just shared, Yohanna raised herself up just enough to lean her arm against his chest and look into Lukkas's eyes.

"So are we still going back to the studio?" she asked, pretending to act as if they hadn't just blown out all the stops and made torrid love together. "Because if the answer's yes, I'm going to need five minutes to pack. Make that ten," she amended, reconsidering, "because I have to put some clothes on first. I don't think your pilot would appreciate my boarding his plane naked."

"I can't see him complaining about that," Lukkas said, playing along. And then he laughed at the absurdity of the conversation. Stroking her hair, which was splayed against his chest, he apologized. "I'm sorry about before."

"Which before?" Yohanna asked cautiously. "Because part of that 'before' was really terrific."

Lukkas was focused on making amends. "I shouldn't have snapped at you like that."

He felt a slight flutter across his skin and realized that she was smiling against his chest. Why that would suddenly make his heart feel full, he had no idea.

"I've endured worse," she told him. "Besides, I'd say that you kind of made up for it." Raising her head again, her eyes met his. Hers twinkled with humor—and maybe a little something more. Whatever it was, it seemed to reel him in.

"I meant what I said the other day, you know," Yohanna told him.

"You said a lot of things on a lot of days," he pointed out, patiently waiting for her to clarify her words.

"You have a point," she conceded. "When I told you that you could talk to me if something were bothering you, I meant it. I really am a good listener and I promise you that whatever you say to me won't go any further than my own ears."

Even though she was trying to have a serious conversation with him, he could feel himself responding to her again. Responding not just to her physically, but to her kindness, her understanding. She was the whole package. Beauty, brains and compassion. And that was rare.

Raising his head a little, he lightly skimmed the tip of his tongue along the outline of her ear. "This ear?" he asked, his warm breath caressing her skin.

She surprised him by maneuvering her body and flipping him onto his back.

"And this ear," she said, turning her head just enough to make her other ear accessible to him.

This time when he mimicked his previous movement, she could feel her whole body responding with a warm shiver that ran the length of it.

She didn't remember all that much immediately after that, except that it was spectacular.

Chapter Fifteen

"So this is the way I find out? When were you going to tell me? Or did you just decide that I didn't need to know?"

Her mother's voice vacillated between sounding indignant and really hurt. Long ago Yohanna had learned that when it came to wielding guilt, her mother was in a class all by herself.

And Elizabeth Andrzejewski had not mellowed with age.

Yohanna frowned. She and Lukkas had returned to Southern California late yesterday. He'd dropped her off at her house while he had gone on to his because he needed to take care of several things.

The blinking light on the answering machine part of her landline had caught her eye the moment she'd entered her house, but for the sake of her own peace of mind, Yohanna had deliberately put off listening to the messages until morning.

Well, now it was morning and here she was listening to her mother lay on the guilt with expert precision. Her mother hadn't been able to reach her while she'd been on location because she'd consciously left her cell phone off. Because unforeseen things had a way of happening, she had left a message on her mother's machine that she was going out of town and couldn't be reached. However, if some kind of *real* emergency came up, her mother could call Lukkas's office at the studio and leave a message. That message would then be forwarded to her as quickly as possible.

Yohanna made sure that her mother would be out having lunch with her friends—something she did every Thursday—before calling. That way she was assured of getting the answering machine. Her reason for this roundabout approach was to avoid fielding the thousand-and-one questions she knew her mother was capable of asking.

The questions that apparently were coming her way now.

"Tell you what, Mom?" Yohanna murmured to her answering machine as it went on playing her mother's far from brief message.

Even though she'd voiced the question out loud, it was purely a rhetorical one. She had a sinking feeling she knew exactly what her mother was referring to and had no doubts that she would be listening to recriminations regarding her "oversight" at length for weeks—possibly months—to come.

The next moment she was proved right. Yohanna took no joy in that.

"You went to a real Hollywood movie premiere with that man, your boss," her mother all but squealed. "Best-looking man you've ever gone out with and did you even *think* to give me a call to let me know? Of course not. I had to find out my daughter was dating a celebrity by watching *Today's Hollywood*," her mother complained bitterly.

"I wasn't 'dating' him, Mother," Yohanna retorted to the answering machine. "I was shielding him."

And now? What are you doing with him now? she asked herself. She honestly didn't have an answer to that, other than the obvious one: that what she was doing with him was having a good time.

"The reporter said that it looked as though Lukkas Spader had finally stopped grieving over his dead wife and was moving on *with his new assistant.* That *is* you, right?" her mother asked with annoyance. "I didn't see anyone else with him in that segment. Just you. My former daughter.

"The woman doing the segment went on to say that you two are an item. An *item.* And you didn't even pick up the phone to tell me, your own *mother.* I raised you better than that. At least I thought I did. Well, let me tell you that is *no way* to treat your long-suffering mother, Yohanna."

Yohanna rolled her eyes. Leaning over the answering machine, she said, "Yes, it is, because I just *knew* you'd be making a big deal out of it. And that's what you're doing," she said, waving a hand at the answering machine. "You're making a big deal out of it."

She sighed, shaking her head. When the time came to actually *talk* to her mother, she knew she wasn't going to say any of what she'd just said, wasn't going to tell her mother to butt out of her affairs—oh, God, her mother would leap on that word, she thought in absolute dismay. No, there would be no indignant comebacks, no angry retorts forthcoming from her.

Instead, she would just sit there, listening to her mother politely, because she would tell herself that, at bottom, her mother meant well and all she *really* wanted for her was just the best.

Meanwhile, her mother thought nothing of making her utterly crazy in the process.

However, her mother and the drama Elizabeth Andrzejewski always created were of secondary importance in the scheme of things. Right now she was far more concerned with what this so-called "breaking news" broadcast her mother had referred to, which she herself as of yet hadn't glimpsed on the air, would do to Lukkas if he happened across it—especially if someone brought it to his attention.

Would the threat of having this labeled a relationship cause him to step back from whatever was building between them? Would he tell her that people would get the wrong idea so to keep things the way they were— professional—he was going to back off?

The very idea of not seeing Lukkas privately anymore felt like a knife to her insides.

But there wasn't anything she could do about that. She was just going to have to be holding her breath until Lukkas found out about the media's current speculation about his life.

Part of her fervently hoped he never would find out because she had a feeling that *that* could very well signal the beginning of the end of their time together. And until just this moment, she hadn't realized that she didn't want it to end. At least not yet.

Not for a while.

A *long* while, she amended.

In all honesty, she had never had a relationship that had actually worked before. There had been a few half-hearted *associations*—for lack of a better word—but they had all simply petered out after a short amount of time.

Maybe it was because, as her mother maintained, she was too picky. But whatever the reason, she had never felt that lighter-than-air feeling she experienced whenever she was with Lukkas. Before she had gone to work for Lukkas, she'd begun to think something was wrong with her. And then she'd met Lukkas and suddenly everything was right with the world.

Her response to Lukkas wasn't just physical—although heaven knew the man, with his well-defined chest, his tight butt and his sleek hips was a feast for the eyes—but he spoke to her on a completely different level.

Spoke to her soul.

Until just recently she had never believed in such things as kindred spirits, never believed in the existence of so-called soul mates. She'd thought it was a term people made up to make themselves feel as if what they had was special and that it would last until the end of time. Usually, it didn't last anywhere nearly as long, and relationship extraction was always rather painful.

But in this case, in *her* case, she felt as if that was exactly what was happening to her. She and Lukkas were quietly building toward something solid. And she wasn't about to have all that work destroyed by some hot-shot

reporter or blogger calling unwanted attention to Lukkas and her, to their association.

She wasn't about to allow Lukkas to be driven away
from her by a few thoughtless words.

When her doorbell rang, she assumed that her mother
had decided to do her "severely wounded mother" act in
person rather than leave another message on the phone.
Since her car was safely put away in the garage, Yohanna
debated pretending she wasn't home.

But her mother was nothing if not persistent. The
doorbell rang a second time. And then a third. This could
go on indefinitely. She might as well get it over with.

Psyching herself up for a confrontation, Yohanna
strode over to the door and yanked it open even as she
started talking quickly. "I didn't tell you anything,
Mother, because there's nothing to tell! Understand?"

"Sure thing."

Her jaw all but dropped when she saw that Lukkas
was standing in her doorway, not her mother.

"Nothing to tell about what, Hanna?" he asked her,
coming in.

She waved away both what she'd said and his question regarding it. "Doesn't matter." She knew she had
to offer him some sort of an explanation in order not to
come off as being too strange. "I came home to half a
dozen messages from my mother. The usual thing," she
told him, brushing the matter aside and hoping he wasn't
going to ask her anything specific about what her mother
had said in those messages.

Hope was short-lived.

"And the usual thing is?" Lukkas asked, attempting
to coax an answer out of her.

Maybe she did need to begin at the beginning. Sort of.

This definitely felt awkward. "One of those red-carpet reporters took a video of you at the premiere."

"You mean of us," Lukkas corrected. He had been quite aware of the clusters of paparazzi that would have been willing to literally kill one another just to get a clear shot of the two of them.

She nodded. "My mother seems to think that I'm keeping something from her."

Pausing for a moment, he took the wildest guess he could. "You mean like a secret wedding?"

She could only stare at him in complete wonder. "What? No. She knows that no matter how crazy she makes me, I wouldn't exclude her from my wedding. That would be too cruel."

Maybe she had said too much. She had a sinking feeling Lukkas was going to say something about nipping this "romance thing" in the bud and that they were going to have to keep everything aboveboard.

"I'm sorry," she told him.

He furrowed his brow. "Did you do something to apologize for?" he asked her.

"No." Technically, she hadn't, Yohanna thought. There was no way she could have foreseen this sort of a reaction from the voyeuristic press.

To her surprise, Lukkas didn't really need any convincing as to her culpability.

"That's right, you didn't. I knew it was a calculated risk, taking you to the premiere to ward off being 'fixed up' by some of my well-meaning friends and their wives." He moved a little closer to her, his eyes holding hers. "What I didn't calculate into this was my own reaction to you."

For a split second her heart almost stopped beating.

"And that is?" Yohanna asked so softly that had he not been standing so close to her, Lukkas wouldn't have even heard the question.

"That you make me feel again. That very possibly you brought that dead part of me back to life. I'm not going to tell you that I'm ready to do cartwheels and break into song right this minute—I've still got issues to work out," he confided. "But you have made me realize that there just might be a light—albeit a very distant light—at the end of this tunnel I'm traveling through."

Her relief was practically immeasurable. "So you're not going to tell me that my services are no longer needed?"

Where had *that* come from?

"You're kidding, right?" he asked her, surprised she would even think something like that.

"No," she admitted. "I was being very serious."

He laughed. "After you made yourself indispensable to me, got the production running like a well-oiled machine—an *efficient*, well-oiled machine—do you actually think I'd stand dramatically in a doorway and point to the road, saying you needed to hit it and never show your face here again?"

It almost sounded melodramatically ludicrous when he said it that way. Still, she wasn't going to lie about her reaction. Maybe he could even say something to make her feel that she wasn't expendable at this time.

"Something like that," she conceded.

"You're just humoring me. You're way too smart to actually think something like that," he told her with finality.

"So what are you going to do about that story the network's running?" When he raised a brow, she understood that he had no idea which story she was referring to. *Nice going, Hanna.* "The one that has us wildly in love," she clarified.

"What I'm going to do is what I've been doing ever since I first started on this pilgrimage to solidly build up my reputation in this otherwise make-believe world of tinsel, smoke and mirrors. I'm going to ignore the story, ignore the paparazzi—a difficult task, but still doable—and go on doing what I'm good at doing. Producing movies people want to see.

"And in order to do that, I intend to keep amassing a production company comprised of people who are damn good at what they do. And that, in case you have any doubts, most assuredly includes you." And then he paused to look at Hanna. He had left out one important point. "Unless, of course, having those stories and the annoying paparazzi swarming around you like so many blood-sucking mosquitoes with cameras is intolerable to you."

His analogy made her smile. "I think that mosquitoes with cameras are rather intriguing. Far be it from me to run for cover. Actually," Yohanna told him proudly, "I've never run from anything in my life."

"With the possible exception of your mother?" It wasn't a contradiction but an amused question on Lukkas's part.

Yohanna inclined her head, conceding the minor point. "I stand corrected. I have run from my mother. But in my defense, I've only run from her because no matter what I say, my mother only hears what she wants to hear—even if what I say isn't anything remotely close to what she wants to hear."

"Well…" he said, thinking that perhaps he had a very

simple solution to her problem. "Would you like me to talk to your mother in this case, straighten things out for you?"

Yohanna wasn't really clear on just exactly what he was offering to "straighten out." Would he tell her mother that they're just sleeping together, thereby minimizing the importance of what they had? Or was he going to tell her mother that they were just friends?

Not that it really mattered. Because either way, her mother would somehow convert the words into what she wanted to hear.

"I think," she began slowly, examining her words very carefully before she uttered them, "for the sake of my continuing to work for you, you should just abandon the idea of talking to my mother, of even saying a single word to her."

"Come again?"

"Talking to my mother might make you want to permanently terminate our association, if only to make sure that there was no reason for you to ever encounter my mother on a one-to-one basis again," she warned him. For once, she didn't feel as if she was exaggerating.

"Get that notion out of your head," he told her. "That's not about to happen, not from my end. There's nothing your mother could possibly do to make me entertain the idea of sending you away so I wouldn't have to deal with her."

In her heart Yohanna felt she knew better. "My mother would have made Gandhi look around for the nearest gun shop."

He laughed. "She can't be *that* bad."

"Trust me, she can. She's not a bad person," Yohanna quickly interjected so that he wouldn't get the wrong idea. Her mother was a peaceful soul—she was just a harpy. "But she can totally make you crazy inside of five minutes. Sometimes less."

Lukkas began to speak, but she held her hand up to silence him. Cornering his attention, she pressed the play button on her answering machine.

"Listen to a couple of her messages and then tell me that she can't be that bad," she told him.

Lukkas dutifully sat on the sofa and listened to the two messages she had already screened.

When she pressed the stop button, Yohanna looked at him, waiting for Lukkas to react. He remained silent for a very long moment. And then he smiled. "I guess you win this round. Apparently your mother *can* be that bad."

"Told you." It gave her no pleasure to be right this time.

"But she's just motivated by her concern for you," he added.

The addendum to his initial appraisal surprised her.

"I do believe you missed your true calling."

He looked at her, puzzled. "What do you mean?"

"You should have joined the diplomatic corps," she told him. "You obviously know how to twist a phrase to make it sound not just good, but like a compliment." Yohanna took a deep breath. She wasn't finished just yet. This was serious. "I could try to get the story squelched."

"You do that," he told her, "and the media'll really feel as if they're on to something. In my experience, you just hang tight and, eventually, the story blows over and something new becomes the focus of every one of those vultures' attention. Big story or little, the one constant is that they all run their course. I wouldn't worry about squelching the story if I were you. The story will die a natural death," he promised.

Still a bit nervous, she ran the tip of her tongue along her lips, trying to moisten them. "So we're okay?" she asked.

The look in her eyes tugged at something he had been so certain he no longer possessed. His heart.

The smile he gave her said it all.

"We're more than okay," Lukkas assured her. "Unless—"

"Unless?" she asked uncertainly.

Here it came. He was going to tell her that if she thought they had a future, then he'd have to bow out because his heart belonged to the woman he'd been forced to bury.

"Unless this is going to scare you away. Every one of those photographers can be pretty intense and intimidating."

"This *definitely* proves you've never met my mother," she told him with a laugh. "You want to talk about being intense and intimidating, my mother is the national poster child."

"I like her already," he said with a laugh.

Getting into the spirit of the situation, Yohanna grinned. "I will remind you of that statement when the times comes."

"You do that, Hanna. But right now, we've got work to do." He rose from the sofa. "Your chariot awaits, milady."

She got up beside him, as well. The feeling of relief she was experiencing was immeasurable. Smiling into his eyes, she laughed and said, "I could *really* get used to this."

Chapter Sixteen

A few days later Lukkas had to leave town on business for a couple of days. He went alone, asking her to "hold down the fort."

She never thought she could miss someone so much.

It felt as if a piece of her—a vital piece—was missing. The only way she knew how to cope with the stark emptiness she felt was to work. Mercifully, there was still a lot to do so she threw herself into it wholeheartedly.

Anything to blot out the ache.

She was so busy prioritizing Lukkas's schedule for his next movie after the present one wrapped, she didn't notice it at first.

But she sensed it.

Sensed someone watching her.

It was actually more of an edgy feeling than anything else. For the most part she dismissed it, telling herself she was beginning to imagine things, the way anyone running on little sleep and dark coffee might after going at her present pace for more than a day.

But there were sounds she *thought* she kept hearing; sounds suspiciously resembling the clicking noise a camera made when a photograph was snapped. But each time she would look up, her gaze sweeping the general area, she wouldn't actually *see* anything that was amiss.

She considered telling Lukkas when he called to see how things were going, but she didn't want him to think she was paranoid. And she definitely didn't want him to worry, so she went on wrestling with this—at present— unsubstantiated feeling that she was being watched, doing her best to talk herself out of it.

Until she finally caught him.

She was being tailed by a freelance photographer.

"Wait!" she cried as he started to run down her block toward a parked car. "I won't call the police," she promised, heading after him. "I just want to know why you've been taking pictures. You've got me confused with someone else. I'm not anybody," she told the scruffy-looking man with the very expensive camera.

Apparently schooled by experience, despite the fact that, for the moment, he stopped running, the man kept a safe distance between them.

"You are to Lukkas Spader. You're the first woman he's been seen with since his wife died—and he's produced movies with some really hot little babes in them. If he thinks you're special, then the public wants to see you. It's that simple."

Raising his camera, he snapped three more shots in incredibly fast succession—and then he took off again, leaving her to ponder his words.

She tried to see his license number, but the plate was obscured.

Was the paparazzo right? she wondered as she returned to her house. *Was* she special to Lukkas? Or was he just with her to help him transition back to the regular world, the world he'd known before he had lost his wife?

She didn't know.

She only knew that she missed Lukkas something awful. Especially at night. Somehow the dark just made the longing worse. Even her own home felt strange to her.

Without Lukkas to fill the spaces of her evening—which she had gotten extremely used to in a short amount of time—her house felt extra empty, extra lonely.

"I need a dog," she said out loud, her voice echoing back at her as she locked the front door, then walked through the house, turning on lights in each room she came to.

She'd put in another extralong day at the studio today, getting everything prepared for Lukkas so when he got back, he would be ready to roll. She absolutely loved the fact that she had gotten really good at anticipating his needs and requirements when it came to working with him.

The other part of it, anticipating his needs as a man... She was more than happy about keeping her finger on *that* particular pulse, as well.

It was past ten o'clock. She was exhausted but too wired to sleep. A vague hunger nudged at her, reminding her that she hadn't eaten very much.

She went into the kitchen and opened her refrigerator. It all but mocked her as she stared unseeingly into its interior.

Nothing seemed to move her or to tempt her taste

buds. There were several things she could whip up—
chicken Parmesan took her less than twenty minutes and
she had both the chicken and the extras that went with
it. But the idea of cooking for herself held absolutely no
appeal for her.

Because she knew she had to eat *something*, Yohanna
took out a cherry-flavored yogurt, uncovered the top and
then, picking up a spoon, started to eat it as she leaned
over the sink.

It took a few moments for the scenario to sink in.
And horrify her.

"My God, I've become one of those women who eats
out of a container while standing over a sink," she muttered, appalled.

She hadn't been like that before Lukkas had entered
her life. She'd been independent and had made her peace
with living a solitary life while making the most of it.
Now all the freedom in the world couldn't begin to make
up for the loneliness that was gnawing away at her.

She missed Lukkas. Missed him so much that it physically hurt.

How had she gotten here? She had absolutely no right
to think that Lukkas was going to be a permanent person in her life. She had to live in the moment, not the
future. Lukkas was kind, handsome, fun and very ap-
proachable. But the man's heart, she sternly reminded
herself, still belonged to his late wife, and if she thought
there was a way she was going to burrow into that heart
and stake a claim to it, then she was going to be horri-
bly disappointed.

She knew that.

Telling herself anything else was just delusional and
putting off the inevitable.

Her spoon hit bottom. Somehow she'd managed to consume the yogurt without even realizing it. Or tasting it.

Listlessly, she threw out the container.

Her landline rang just then. She instantly brightened, pushing aside the darkness that threatened to swallow her up.

Yohanna pulled the receiver out of the cradle and put it to her ear. At this point she'd even welcome a call from her mother. Anything to keep her mind from sliding back down into the darkness.

She yanked the receiver up so quickly, she didn't even look at the name on the small screen identifying the caller.

"Hello?"

"How's everything going?"

Her face broke out in a wreath of smiles. Lukkas's voice had a way of reassuring her.

She dutifully gave him a quick summary. "The schedule's coming together. Everything's going to be ready for your review when you get back." Which she hoped was going to be sometime tomorrow—the sooner the better.

"Are you sure about that?"

She thought that was rather an odd statement to make—he didn't usually question what she said—but she gave him the reassurance he was looking for. "I wouldn't tell you if I wasn't," she pointed out.

"What if I get back early?"

Oh, please get back early, she silently prayed. "It's actually ready right now, so you can come back anytime you want," she told him.

"Sounds good," he told her.

The doorbell rang just then.

"What's that noise?" Lukkas asked.

"That's just someone at the door." She was perfectly willing to ignore whoever was there since the most important person in her world was on the phone with her.

"Aren't you going to answer it?" Lukkas asked her.

"I'm busy," she told him, her voice soft and low. "Talking to you." The doorbell rang again, splicing into her sentence.

"Whoever it is sounds as if they're going to be persistent," Lukkas observed, and then advised, "Maybe you should call your security service, just in case there's a problem."

"I don't have a security service," she reminded him.

She closed her eyes as the doorbell rang yet again. There was only one person who didn't give up after a couple of tries.

"It's probably my mother," she said with a sigh. "Hold on."

With that, still holding the receiver in her hand, she went to the front door and opened it.

"I'm not your mother," Lukkas said, closing the cell phone he had in his hand.

She let her portable receiver slip through her fingers. It fell on the floor. She hardly noticed. Overjoyed that he'd come back early, she threw her arms around Lukkas.

"What are you doing here?" she cried.

"Currently?" he asked with a straight face. "Having the air squeezed out of my lungs," he answered with a laugh.

Suddenly realizing that her arms had all but tightened into a viselike grip, she loosened her hold on him.

"Don't take this the wrong way, because I'm thrilled to have you back, but what happened? You weren't supposed to be back for at least one more day, if not more," she told him.

Lukkas shrugged. "I cut myself a little slack. You're so efficient that I figured I could do that once in a while. Besides, I missed you," he told her.

As he began to lower his mouth to hers, he stopped abruptly when he saw them. "Hey, what's this? Tears?" he asked incredulously, lightly touching the damp path the tear had created. "I didn't say that to make you cry."

"Too late," she told him. Up on her toes, she pulled him closer and covered his lips with her own.

Lukkas meant to only kiss her lightly before he told her why he'd *really* cut things short and flown back earlier than planned. But when she kissed him like that, it felt as if everything inside him just began to radiate, to glow.

Accustomed to flying here, there and everywhere at the drop of a hat, fitting in all those different places, belonging nowhere, he hadn't experienced a feeling of homecoming for years now.

"Home" was everywhere and nowhere—until now.

Now *she* was home, he realized. Hanna was his go-to place. His haven.

But all of this hit him afterward. After he had kissed her until his lips were all but numb. After he'd savored every inch of her and made love with her not once, but twice.

Gloriously.

Recklessly.

Lying in her bed, holding her to him, Lukkas searched for the right words to convey all this to her. This and more.

But just when he needed it most, eloquence escaped him.

"I know it's only been a few days, but I've missed

you," he told her, murmuring the words softly into her hair. At first he thought she hadn't heard him, but then he felt her curl farther into him, her arm across his chest tightening.

He felt his whole body quicken in response.

"I missed you, too," she told him, her words floating on her warm breath and skimming across his skin.

He wanted her all over again.

Lukkas struggled to hold himself in check. He needed to get something out in the open first.

"Then, why didn't you call?" he asked. "You didn't even call when you had updates for me."

He'd had to be the one to call, making him feel that he needed her more than she needed him.

"I texted them," she pointed out. "And I didn't want to bother you—or to sound needy," she finally admitted.

"You wouldn't have bothered me," he told her, wondering where she had gotten that impression. "And I really doubt you could sound needy even if you tried."

She was strong and forceful—and soft in all the right places, he couldn't help thinking.

"Oh, you'd be surprised," Yohanna told him.

She'd worried about that more than once—that he would see how much she cared about him, how much she wanted to be part of his life. Because of his past and what the loss of his wife had done to him, she was afraid that he would see her behavior as encroaching on him and he would wind up severing all ties with her.

She didn't know if she could bear that, even if, ultimately, Lukkas had done it for his own good. She wasn't that selfless, even if she wanted to be.

"Does that mean you'd miss me if I were gone?"

Lukkas's question brought her up out of her thoughts with a thud.

It sounded like an innocent question, but she had learned that nothing was really all that innocent.

Feeling as if she was walking on a thin, scarred wooden plank stretched over a bed of quicksand where one misstep would make her disappear, she asked him quietly, "Are you going somewhere?"

Lukkas continued to play devil's advocate. "If I was, how would you feel about it?" he asked. "Would you ask me not to go?"

Her first reaction was that she wouldn't ask him not to go, she'd beg him not to. But she couldn't say that; she didn't have the right.

And, after a moment, that was what she told him, as well.

"If you wanted to go, I wouldn't have the right to ask you not to."

"But if you did have the right?" he asked, continuing to play out the line, waiting for her to tell him what he wanted to hear.

She was doing her best to hold her emotions in check. To be his assistant, not the woman who was in love with him.

"I'd want you to be happy. If going made you happy, then I wouldn't stop you."

Lukkas continued watching her face, searching it for a sign. "So what you're telling me is that you're indifferent," he concluded.

She knew what she was supposed to say, what she *should* say as his assistant, which was the only official position she held. But despite that, something within her just couldn't allow her to continue with the charade she was playing.

"I am *so* not indifferent," she said, contradicting his conclusion.

The look in his eyes seemed to urge her on, so even though she was certain she was probably destroying the tiny piece of paradise she was temporarily claiming as her own, she told Lukkas exactly what was in her heart.

"If I could, I'd ask you—beg you, really—to stay because when you're gone, nothing makes sense to me. I know I've spent the first thirty years of my life without you and I functioned just fine like that. I got through one end of the day to the other, accomplishing whatever it was I was supposed to accomplish. But now everything's changed. All I can think of is how many minutes before I can see you again, before you kiss me again. Before we make the world stand still again.

"I know this isn't what you probably want to hear and I promise I won't try to hold you back when you want to go—but please don't want to go," she pleaded quietly. "Not yet."

He laughed then, and she didn't know if she was on solid ground or if what she'd just said had struck him as ridiculously funny.

All she could do was ask.

"Why are you laughing?" she asked when he continued chuckling to himself.

It took him a second to catch his breath. "Call your mother," he told her.

She stared at him, certain she must have heard wrong. "What?"

"Call your mother," Lukkas repeated, this time far more audibly.

She could see him asking her to do a great many things for him. But never once would she have thought he would tell her to call her mother, especially after what she had told him about her.

"Why?" she asked in hushed disbelief. "Why would you want me to call my mother, of all people?" That, in her book, was akin to having a death wish.

"So you can tell her she can stop trying to set you up with her friends' sons and nephews. Tell her your fiancé doesn't like it."

Her mouth dropped open and she stared at Lukkas in total disbelief. Now she knew she *had* to be dreaming— or at least hallucinating. But she hadn't ingested anything that even remotely had those side effects.

"My what?"

"Fiancé." And then it hit him. He'd left parts out.

"I'm getting ahead of myself, aren't I?" It was a rhetorical question. "I'm assuming you're going to say yes, and I didn't mean to do that. Of course, if you say no, it'll shatter me after I spent all this time looking for— Oh, damn," he muttered as another thought hit him.

"Oh, damn what?"

Instead of answering, Lukkas sat up and looked around the room. Spotting what he was looking for, his jacket, which was on the floor right next to the bed, he leaned over to pluck it up and pull it onto the bed.

Feeling the pocket, he detected the slight bulge and smiled his relief.

"Still here."

Before she could ask Lukkas what he was talking about, he took a small black velvet box out of the pocket, flipped it open with his thumb and held it out to her.

"Hanna, you brought the sunshine back into my life and I don't want to go back to living in the dark."

He took a breath and said the most important words of his life—for a second time. "Will you marry me?"

For the second time, her mouth dropped open. She looked at Lukkas, then at the ring and back again.

"You're serious?"

Lukkas laughed shortly. "I'm naked, holding a ring, with my entire life riding on your answer. This is about as vulnerable as I can get. So yes, I'm serious." He took her free hand into his as he made his case. "I didn't think I could love anyone ever again, or *risk* loving anyone again.

"But you, just by being you, showed me that I could, that my life had meaning again and that it was time to stop sleepwalking through each day. I can't take the ring back, so it's yours no matter what your answer is, but I'm hoping that you'll take me along with it, although—"

Stifling a laugh, Yohanna put her finger against his lips, momentarily silencing him.

"I never thought I would ever hear myself saying this to you, but shut up, Lukkas. You're talking too much and it's not necessary. That's a lot of wasted rhetoric. I've been yours from the very first day."

He still wasn't going to take anything for granted. "Then it's yes? I want to be clear on this," he specified.

"It's *always* been yes," she said.

The phone rang just as he reached for her again. Glancing at the phone's caller ID, she groaned, then picked up the receiver. "Can't talk right now. I'm getting married, Mom. Call you back later." With that, she hung up and looked at her husband-to-be.

"Where were we?"

"Here, I think," he said, pulling her into his arms.

The phone rang again just as he was going to begin kissing her. He intended to create a path that ran the length and breadth of her body.

They ignored the ringing phone.

She would get back to her mother eventually, Yohanna thought. But right at this moment there was something far more important on her mind. She wanted to make love with her fiancé for the very first time.

And she did.

Epilogue

"You really have outdone yourself, you know," Maizie whispered to Theresa as wedding guests filed into the rows of seats that had been set up in the garden behind the hotel.

Theresa was catering yet another affair for Lukkas Spader. This time, though, it was his wedding, and she had pulled out all the stops.

"Using the red carpet to designate the aisle that the bride comes down was truly a stroke of genius," Maizie told her with admiration.

"It just seemed fitting," Theresa replied in the same hushed tone.

Satisfied that everything was running smoothly and that her employees had everything under control, Theresa had allowed herself a small island of time to simply enjoy being a spectator at another one of their success stories.

So far, she, Maizie and Cecilia, in their capacity as Matchmaking Mamas, were batting a thousand.

"From what Cecilia told me, it seems as if Lukkas first fell in love with Yohanna when they attended the premiere of his movie. I saw that photograph one of those awful pushy paparazzi people had taken of the two of them in a weekly magazine. Lukkas had a smitten face if ever I saw one."

Standing beside the two women in the second-to-last row of folding chairs at the outdoor wedding, Cecilia could only agree with her best friends. But she also had a footnote to offer.

"You want to see smitten, take a look at the bride's mother. That woman looks as if she's just died and gone to heaven." Cecilia nodded at a striking woman in blue standing at the rear of the gathering, just in front of the hotel door.

Maizie glanced in Elizabeth Andrzejewski's direction. The woman was positively beaming. "She certainly does look very proud," she agreed.

"Of herself," Cecilia exhorted. "She's telling anyone she can corner that *she* was the one who was responsible for bringing all this around."

"You're kidding," Theresa said, surprised.

"No, I'm not. According to her, she had kept after Yohanna, urging her to go out with her 'handsome boss' until the girl finally did." Cecilia laughed as she shook her head.

"Ladies, be kind," Maizie told her friends, then winked to cast a smidgeon of doubt on her sincerity in this matter. "We all remember what that was like, desperately wanting to see each of our daughters get married to a good man."

"Yes, but we didn't nag them," Cecilia pointed out.

"Actually, we did—if you ask the girls," Theresa reminded her.

Cecilia shrugged off Theresa's words. "Anyway, that's all in the past," she said with a careless wave of her hand.

Maizie looked at the groom, who was standing beside his best man, anxiously glancing toward the rear of the hotel where the bride was getting ready.

"Nice to see another happy couple preparing to spend the rest of their lives together," Maizie commented with an approving smile.

Just then, the orchestra ceased tuning up. Half a second of silence then gave way to the beginning strains of the "Wedding March."

All conversation ceased as the wedding guests turned almost in unison to look to the rear, waiting for Yohanna to emerge from the hotel.

The hush intensified as the guests watched Yohanna walk down the aisle, which was, in this case, the red carpet Theresa had pulled strings to acquire for the occasion.

Initially, Yohanna had been going to walk to the altar alone since her father had died a long time ago and she'd felt the position belonged to him exclusively. But, at the last minute, she changed her mind and asked her rather stunned mother to accompany her on the symbolic walk.

She told her mother it was only right, since the woman had so anxiously wanted to give her away for the past ten years.

"I just wanted you to have someone to love," Elizabeth told her. "Like I had."

"I know, Mom. I know," Yohanna told her, linking her arm with her mother's when the orchestra began to play.

Elizabeth was positively beaming as she walked beside her daughter. She loved to focus on the fact that she was giving her daughter away to Lukkas Spader, a man who was not only good-looking, famous and well-off, but just possibly was the nicest son-in-law on the face of the earth. This was the way she described Lukkas to each one of her friends, all of whom had been invited to the wedding and reception.

Walking down the red carpet, Elizabeth was in her glory. It was an event that she would remember for the rest of her life no matter how long she lived. She said as much, in a hushed whisper, to her daughter. Then followed that up with a question.

"Do you love him, baby?" Elizabeth asked when they were almost at the flower-laden altar that had been built less than a day earlier by some of the scenery crew who had worked on Lukkas's last movie. A fact that Elizabeth would proudly repeat a dozen times over to her friends at the reception, as well.

Yohanna's eyes were on Lukkas, her heart swelling with each step she took that brought her closer to him. "Very, very much," she answered.

"Then, my job here is done," her mother announced, all but bursting with pride.

"Yes, it is, Mom," Yohanna told her with no small relief.

They came to a stop right beside Lukkas. "You're so beautiful it hurts," he whispered to his wife-to-be, a deep smile curving his lips.

Yohanna blushed.

"Who gives this woman away?" the minister asked.

"I do!" Elizabeth cried loudly enough to be heard not

just in the last row but quite possibly inside the hotel lobby, as well.

Lukkas and Yohanna, who only had eyes for one another, were quite possibly the only two people who hadn't heard Elizabeth's loud declaration. The couple was too busy listening intently to the words the minister was saying.

The words that would forever bind them to one another.

It couldn't happen soon enough for either of them.

* * * * *

Don't miss Marie Ferrarella's next romance,
HOW TO SEDUCE A CAVANAUGH,
available July 2015 from
Harlequin Romantic Suspense!

#2413 The Maverick's Accidental Bride
Montana Mavericks: What Happened at the Wedding?
by Christine Rimmer

Childhood pals Will Clifton and Jordyn Leigh Cates rekindle their friendship over punch at a summer wedding. That's the last thing they remember, and then they wake up married! As they puzzle out the circumstances of their nuptials, Will realizes that beautiful Jordyn—his *wife*—is all grown up. The rancher is determined to turn their "marriage" into reality and hold on to Jordyn's love...forever!

#2414 The Lawman Lassoes a Family
Conard County: The Next Generation • by Rachel Lee

Widow and single mother Vicki Templeton is new to Conard County, Wyoming. She's hoping for a second chance at life with her daughter. Little does she expect another shot at love, too, in the form of her next-door neighbor, Deputy Sheriff Dan Casey. He's also grieving the past, but Dan, Vicki and her little girl might just find their future as a family on the range.

#2415 The M.D.'s Unexpected Family
Rx for Love • by Cindy Kirk

Single dad Dr. Tim Duggan has his hands full with his twin daughters. The last thing he needs is a lovely woman distracting him from fatherhood and his job. But irrepressible Cassidy Kaye finds her way into his arms and his heart. After the hairstylist winds up pregnant, Tim's determined to make the bubbly beauty part of his family forever.

#2416 How to Marry a Doctor
Celebrations, Inc. • by Nancy Robards Thompson

Anna Adams knows her best friend, Dr. Jake Lennox, can't find a girlfriend to save his life. So she offers to set him up on five dates to find The One. Jake decides to find the perfect guy for Anna, as well...until he realizes that the only one he wants in Anna's arms is himself! Can the good doc diagnose a case of happily-ever-after—for himself and the alluring Anna?

#2417 Daddy Wore Spurs
Men of the West • by Stella Bagwell

When horse trainer Finn Calhoun learns he might be the father to a baby boy, he gallops off to Stallion Canyon, a ranch in northern California, to find out the truth. The infant's aunt and guardian, Mariah Montgomery, tries to resist the cowboy's charm, but this trio might just find the happiest ending in the West!

#2418 His Proposal, Their Forever
The Coles of Haley's Bay • by Melissa McClone

Artist Bailey Cole loves working at the local inn in Haley's Bay, Washington...but a very handsome, very dangerous threat looms. The hunky hotelier's name is Justin McMillian, and he's about to buy out Bailey's dreams from under her. As stubborn Bailey and sexy Justin butt heads over the project, then find common ground, sparks fly and kindle flames of true love.

HSECNM0615

Then, of course, there was Dan, who was still holding her
hand as if it were the most ordinary thing in the world. Once
again she noticed the warmth of his palm clasped to hers, the
strength of the fingers tangled with hers. Damn, something
about him called to her, but it could never be, simply because
he was a cop.

"I'm not making you feel smothered, am I?"

Startled, she looked at him. "No. How could you think
that? You've been helpful, but you haven't been hovering."

He laughed quietly. "Good. When you first arrived I had
two thoughts. You're Lena's niece, and I'm crazy about Lena,
so I wanted to make you feel at home. The second was…wait
for it…"

"Duty," she answered. "Caring for the cop's widow and kid."

She didn't know whether to laugh or cry. It was everywhere.

"Of course," he answered easily. "Nothing wrong with it. Even around here where the job is rarely dangerous, we all like knowing that we can depend on the others to keep an eye on our families. Nothing wrong with that. But I can see how it might go too far. And everyone's different, with different needs."

She sidestepped a little to avoid a place where the sidewalk was cracked and had heaved up. His hand seemed to steady her.

"Promise me something," he said.

"If I can."

"If I start to smother you, you'll tell me. I wouldn't want to do that."

"I'm not sure you could," she answered honestly. "But I promise."

He seemed to hesitate, very unlike him. "There was a third reason I wanted to help out," he said slowly.

"What was that?"

He surprised her. He stopped walking, and when she turned to face him, he took her gently by the shoulders. Before she understood what he was doing, he leaned in and kissed her lightly on the lips. Just a gentle kiss, the merest touching of their mouths, but she felt an electric shock run through her, felt something long quiescent spring to heated life.

Love the Harlequin book you just read?

Your opinion matters.

Review this book on your favorite book site, review site, blog or your own social media properties and share your opinion with other readers!

JUST CAN'T GET ENOUGH?

Join our social communities
and talk to us online.

You will have access to the latest
news on upcoming titles and special
promotions, but most importantly,
you can talk to other fans about your
favorite Harlequin reads.

Harlequin.com/Community

 Facebook.com/HarlequinBooks

 Twitter.com/HarlequinBooks

Pinterest.com/HarlequinBooks

HARLEQUIN®

A Romance FOR EVERY MOOD™

**Stay up-to-date on all your
romance-reading news with the
Harlequin Shopping Guide,
featuring bestselling authors, exciting new
miniseries, books to watch and more!**

The newest issue will be delivered right to you
with our compliments! There are 4 each year.

Signing up is easy.

EMAIL

ShoppingGuide@Harlequin.ca

WRITE TO US

HARLEQUIN BOOKS
Attention: Customer Service Department
P.O. Box 9057, Buffalo, NY 14269-9057

OR PHONE

1-800-873-8635 in the United States
1-888-343-9777 in Canada

Please allow 4-6 weeks for delivery of the first issue by mail.

THE WORLD IS BETTER WITH

Romance

Harlequin has everything from contemporary, passionate and heartwarming to suspenseful and inspirational stories.

Whatever your mood,
we have a romance just for you!

Connect with us to find your next great read,
special offers and more.

f /HarlequinBooks

🐦 @HarlequinBooks

www.HarlequinBlog.com

www.Harlequin.com/Newsletters

 HARLEQUIN®

A *Romance* FOR EVERY MOOD™

www.Harlequin.com